Mt. Everest IN FLIP-FLOPS

Terence Shannon

Mt. Everest in Flip-Flops
Copyright 2018 Terence Shannon
All rights reserved.
ISBN-13: 978-0-9679206-2-7
Edited by Todd Larson/thewriter
Cover design by Cosqai LTD
Interior art by Amy Layton/TrueForm Graphics
Interior Layout: Laura Shinn Designs

Other books by this author:
What Happened to the Indians

Mt. Everest in Flip-Flops is a work of fiction. Though some of the cities and towns actually exist they are used in a fictitious manner for purposes of this work. All characters are works of fiction and any names or characteristics similar to any person past, present or future are coincidental.

For Michele

Chapter One

In 1972, when I was nineteen, I took a job as a counselor at a summer camp run by the Catholic Church. I spent seventy-six days and nights there—I know the exact number, because the Monday morning I arrived and the Saturday I left at noon are among my most memorable days. In some manner, I have never left the place, nor has it ever left me. Due to circumstances of fate, I could have told this story long before now. When I retired, I thought I might write about it as a kind of therapy. I didn't. My wife knows the story and wants me to tell it.

So why am I choosing to do it now? In my years on the bench I sentenced six men to die. None have been executed, but, for one, the days are dwindling, and the closer it gets, the more it draws me back to that summer place almost fifty years ago.

Fort Ross was a considerable operation—over a thousand acres surrounded by rolling green farmland. About half the property was thickly wooded. The other half was grass upon which sat about sixty buildings for the camp. All buildings were painted white and wood-framed with green-shingled roofs, except for the chapel, which was red brick. About forty of the buildings were cabins big enough for nine kids and a counselor, each containing five bunkbeds. Two massive mess halls accommodated two hundred fifty campers and counselors apiece. There was a boys' camp and a girls' camp, so there were two Olympic-sized swimming pools. The stable boasted forty horses.

That first Monday I arrived as part of a crew to get the camp ready and settled in the boys' shack, where the thirty or so guys who weren't counselors lived. Just a few of the bunks were occupied; I had taken the next open one down. I was unpacking my stuff temporarily there when I heard a vehicle pull up. Then Dalton Talbott came in. He was three years older than me, starting his last year in college. He was tall and blonde and wearing high-top leather workboots. His eyes were strikingly blue. He had a straight nose, a square jaw, and an air of confidence and ease. His face had a friendliness to which smiles came naturally.

Dalton was wearing a wry smile as he approached me, introduced himself, and asked if I was here for pre-camp maintenance. When I told him I was, he laughed a little. "Put some jeans on, Jake," he told me. "I know it's going to be hot as hell today. But put them on anyway to start out. We got a job to do."

"What?"

"Under the girls' mess hall there are storage cellars with sacks of government flour and grain. Rats got into them over the winter."

"Rats?" My eyes about popped out of my head. "How many rats?"

"I don't know. About fifty to a hundred. I didn't count them. They're crawling all over the place."

"We're going to kill them?"

"Well, we're not going to let them loose. Come on, it'll be fun."

That was my introduction to Fort Ross. I should say here that I have a particular aversion to rats. And why absolutely everyone else doesn't is a profound mystery to me. In a room full of women, I'd be the first one jumping up on a chair, but I couldn't say that. I started looking for jeans that were still in my duffel bag.

I heard another vehicle pull up. Stevie and Uncle Bob came in. Dalton was head of the maintenance department; Stevie and Uncle Bob filled it out. Maintenance was responsible for cutting grass mostly, but also for fixing screens and pipes and anything else that went wrong with sixty-odd buildings. Stevie and Uncle Bob were both twenty. Stevie was short and strong; Uncle Bob was a little heavy and moved kind of slowly. I never knew, and never asked, why they called him Uncle Bob, but everyone did. He was 'Uncs' for short. They both wore green John Deere hats. They lived nearby and worked during the year for Charlie, the ailing caretaker of the camp, while attending college.

The four of us sat on our cots and changed into jeans. We were the only four beds taken in a fairly cavernous place. Dalton had a big corner with a ratty overstuffed chair and a light over it. Everyone else had just a metal locker. Dalton had one of those, and an old dresser, too, with pictures on it.

With his jeans on, Dalton moved to the overstuffed chair to put on his leather boots. A stand-alone ashtray lay beside the chair. He lit a cigarette. "You want one, Jake?"

"No."

"Come on. They're good for you. They're good for killing rats."

Stevie and Uncle Bob had brought with them a big roll of white masking tape. We wrapped it around the bottoms of our jeans and joined them to our shoes. I didn't have leather workboots like the others, but I did have a pair of high-top Converse sneakers—no rat was going to go up my pants. From the shins downward, I looked ready to play a game in the NFL.

Finally, Dalton took the roll of tape from me, for I would never have finished.

"Hey, Dalton," I said.

"What?"

"These rats you're talking about—are they *real* rats, or pretend rats?"

We all started laughing. It was clear that Stevie and Uncle Bob didn't want any part of this, either. "Jake, some of them are as big as raccoons," Dalton said.

We discussed strategy. Stevie favored using flat-headed shovels to cut the rats in two. Uncle Bob suggested a flat-headed gravel rake to grind them into the concrete floor. I wasn't saying much now, trying to keep from throwing up. Dalton brightened my mood a little when he brought up defense. His idea was to use stiff brooms to control the varmints, to keep them away from and off of us if we needed to.

Dalton stood alone. Stevie and Uncle Bob were still glued to their cots, as I was. "Come on," Dalton said. "Put your purses down and let's do this. Come on. It'll be fun."

"Hey, Dalton," I said.

"What?"

"Give me a cigarette." We all started laughing again. "Sit down." I motioned him with my forefinger. "I'm smoking a cigarette first."

Dalton got a kick out of it. He sat back down, more than happy to grant me my last wish. It was the first cigarette I ever had. I coughed at first, but I liked it. I was definitely experiencing a nicotine high as we strode out of the boys' shack together.

I rode with Dalton in his blue Ford Pickup truck to the barn. I can't remember what year the truck was, from the 1930s. It was a beat-up wreck that never left the grounds, no doors, rusting out. Charlie made sure the engine ran, though. It purred. Stevie and Uncle Bob shared a white pickup truck that was slightly newer than Dalton's but had none of the character of his. Maintenance never walked anywhere. The only time Dalton walked *anywhere* at Fort Ross was with a girl. And you always knew where he was by where his truck was parked.

The barn was something of an icon. As you entered into the property, and before you saw either camp, you went straight up a steady hill, and at the top was a big barn, glistening white, with 'FORT ROSS' in bold black letters. It was a working barn—Charlie baled hay there, among other agricultural pursuits: he had about a ten-acre cornfield, and he raised pigs and grazed cows. Stevie and Uncle Bob did all of it for him now, for Charlie was an old man in poor health. His wife, Rose, had passed two years prior.

At the barn we sharpened three flat-headed shovels until they were razor-like, and we collected two gravel rakes and two stiff brooms. In the shed Stevie pick up a stray golf club, an iron, and stepped outside to give it a trial swing. I didn't think much of the idea, and neither did Dalton, though he swung it, too, and then looked at the bottom of the club to see what number it was. "Try it if you want," he said, handing it back to Stevie. "Even God can't hit a two-iron."

With Dalton in the lead truck and me riding shotgun, we went down the hill from the barn and approached the girls' mess hall. Another wave of nausea was roiling through my stomach. Since the truck had no doors, I half-considered rolling out.

Lil, the head cook, came running out the kitchen door before we could turn off our engines. She was a tall, slender woman in her fifties with a black bouffant hairstyle that threatened low-hanging tree limbs. "Get every last one, Dalton," she said. "Every last one."

"Consider it done, Lil," Dalton replied breezily.

"I'll have a good lunch waiting for you boys." (I was wondering if I would still be alive when lunch rolled around.)

The storage rooms were accessed by concrete steps leading down about a ten-foot drop to a concrete floor. We lined up with our bellies on the protective rail as we looked down into the stairwell. There were three metal doors. In the middle of the floor was a drain. The whole lower structure appeared to be concrete, I noted. There would be no route for the rats to get away, unless we marched them up the steps. Which meant they were trapped, and so was I.

"We'll do the middle room first," Dalton said. "There's not that many in there."

We took down all our implements, including the golf club, and two steel garbage cans. No one was doing any talking now. Dalton pulled open the middle door; right away a squeaking noise came from inside. My heart pounded frantically in my chest.

"Do they sound pretend, Jake?" Dalton asked.

We had enough sunlight to see to the back wall. In fact, the morning sun was streaming in. I didn't allow myself to look down at the floor. I looked in the room only enough to determine its size—about fifteen feet deep and ten feet wide.

The sacks of food rested on two skids. With a gravel rake Dalton snagged the first one and drew it just a couple of feet to the doorway. We unloaded the sacks, which were still mostly full, and then drew the skid out. We repeated it for the second skid.

"All right, guys," Dalton declared, "it's show-time."

Of course, we had no idea what we were doing, but at the barn we had decided to go in with one shovel, one rake and two brooms. I thought that wise—play some defense until we knew what we were dealing with. Dalton wanted the flat-headed shovel, Stevie the rake. Uncle Bob and I would man the brooms. We figured the rats would stay against the walls more than come at us, so we decided the brooms should be on the outside of the brigade.

Dalton went in first; I was last. We stepped into about an inch of flour and grain scattered on the floor. At the base of the back wall, about ten rats were moving around with agitation but staying against the wall. A couple were big and fat with thick brown hair and long tails. Others weren't that big. As if we were gunfighters at the O.K. Corral, we started to move slowly forward in a line. Dalton was to my right with the razor-sharp shovel. As we proceeded, the squeaking intensified, but we kept our steady pace.

When we were about five feet away from the rats, they massed mostly in one corner on my side. Dalton thrust his shovel into the pack and probably sliced two or three of them into parts with a single blow. Of the six or seven in our corner, two tried to make a run for it before Dalton could land his shovel again. One stayed on the wall. I let that one go momentarily and took care of the one headed at Dalton, swishing him back into the corner where Dalton was making mincemeat. I got the one against the wall, too—a small one—back into the bloody pile.

Stevie must have made quick work on his side, because he started to grind them with his gravel rake on our side. That rake was quite effective, too: we killed eleven rats in under a minute, I would say. Not all were dead, I don't think, but we shoveled them into the garbage can. Rat blood was all over the place in the corners, especially on my side—I could smell it.

"All right, boys," Dalton said. "One down. Two to go. This is a day at the beach."

When Dalton pulled open the second door, the squeaking was about twice as loud, or louder.

"Hey, Dalton," I said. "Are there any lifeguards at this beach?"

This time it was Stevie who dragged the skids to the doorway with a gravel rake. After unloading the sacks and drawing out the skids, we lined up again the same way. About twenty-five rats were squirming over each other against the back wall. They were of all sizes: big, middling, small. We approached them at the same pace as the first round. This time, when we neared them, they split about evenly into the two back corners. Dalton jammed his shovel into the mass and must have wounded at least five or six. This time four took off from the group at the first hit, and there was no way we could control all of them. I got the one headed at Dalton, and that was it. At least three went out the door, and another shot out of the bloody mess I missed with my swipe against the wall.

The same thing must have happened on the other side, because about ten rats had scampered outside when the carnage inside was finished. They weren't trying for the steps—just running around on the concrete floor of the well. We worked more as two teams outside, Dalton and me, Stevie and Uncle Bob. With a broom and a good weapon we were able to trap and catch them and shovel them all into the garbage can without counting.

After that we took a short break and sat down on the steps. Dalton lit a cigarette and asked me if I wanted one. "When this thing is over with," I said.

When Dalton pulled open the third door, the squeaking came forth with an intensity I can still hear today. By now I considered myself an expert on the decibel level of agitated rats. I knew there had to be close to half a hundred in there.

"Are we still at the beach?" I asked.

We dragged the skids to the doorway. Some of these sacks were almost consumed—mostly paper. As we drew out the second skid, a big bull rat charged at us, its white teeth showing. We weren't expecting it, and it got to within a couple feet of us when Stevie smashed it into the concrete with the gravel rake he was using to drag the skids.

"We need to get them out here," Dalton said. "Two of us should go inside with the brooms and scare some out." It sounded like a decent plan, until he turned to me and asked, "You ready, Jake?"

I was. I don't know how or why I was, but I was. "What the hell," I said. "Let's do it."

As Dalton and I stepped inside with brooms, another rat charged—a particularly fat one. We both got a broom on it and shoved it out the door where Stevie and Uncle Bob were waiting. They both got a piece of it, too, with the shovel and the rake. That was one dead fat bloody rat.

There were no more direct charges, for Dalton and I had kind of figured out how to herd them. Thankfully, they stayed mainly against the walls. Dalton would separate five or ten at a time while I protected him from minor forays. Then we joined Stevie and Uncle Bob outside to take care of them.

It took a while, maybe a half hour, to finish the last room. When about ten rats were left inside, we lined up as we started out and marched toward the back wall with the brooms on the outside. I told Dalton I wanted the shovel and took it from him, giving him my broom. "See, Jake," he said as we switched places, "didn't I tell you this was going to be fun?"

When we were finished, we had a full steel garbage can of dead or mostly-dead rats, which Dalton and I carried up the steps. It weighed a ton. We lifted it to the bed of Dalton's blue Ford Pickup and placed it next to the food sacks we had already carefully carried up. They were still mostly intact. "Charlie's pigs are going to be eating good," Dalton said.

Cleaning up took a little while, too. The second garbage can we filled with the flour and grain from the concrete floor—a pretty disgusting combination of food, rat blood and rat crap. Then we hosed the whole place down. Luckily, the floor had a drain, and it didn't clog, despite all the stuff we were shooting down it.

Dalton and I drove back together to the barn. We stored the food, and then there were the garbage cans to take care of. I sat in the truck looking at the barn while Dalton went back inside to retrieve a gasoline can. The barn truly was an impressive structure, with a concrete block foundation and two sliding doors on the front that were perhaps fifteen feet high. The barn looked as though they painted it every year, because it was bright white. A picture of it was used prominently in any promotion of the camp.

We drove maybe thirty feet from the barn and stopped at the pigpen. The pigs rushed to the trough that was right at the fence, snorting and squealing—maybe forty of them. When Dalton and I got out and unloaded the garbage can, the noise got even louder. Then Dalton raised an arm to the sky, and the pigs shut up immediately. It was instantaneous. Dalton turned to me and smiled. Once they were quiet, we lifted the can half over the fence and dumped its disgusting contents into the trough. Then there were plenty of grunts again. For a moment we watched them munching. "I can't believe you're feeding them that," I said. "And I can't believe they're eating it."

Dalton wasn't concerned. "Pigs'll eat doorknobs."

I just shook my head. "I never want to eat any of *these* pigs."

Dalton laughed.

At the dump we poured out a two-to-three-foot-high mound of bloody rats. I didn't see any still moving. Dalton doused the pile with a liberal amount of gasoline and threw a lit pack of matches onto it. What followed were a bright flash, a loud pop, and the putrid smell of rat hair burning.

"You ready for that cigarette?" Dalton asked me.

"Yeah."

At lunch the kitchen staff treated us like conquering heroes. Dalton formally introduced me to Lil. "He's a good guy," Dalton said about me. I was surprised by this, and pleased.

We were late for lunch in the boys' mess hall, so it was just the four of us. Maintenance was allowed to be late. No one else would think of going back in the kitchen to wash their hands before a meal. Maintenance did it routinely.

Sitting across from Dalton at lunch, I studied him. He was a decent-looking guy, but it was his personality that was so attractive. His blue eyes gleamed with a happy boyish optimism. There was something absolutely positive about him. He acted as if he were sole heir to some vast fortune. Which he was, but in a pleasant sort of way—the way someone with that kind of money *should* act.

I didn't know it then, but Dalton was from an extremely wealthy family. It surprised me when I found out that first week. I had seen him fix screens and toilets and lawnmowers. Dalton never said a word about his money. Everybody else did. Just about everyone who worked at Fort Ross was of some money, but Dalton was from *real* money.

After lunch, we drove back to the boys' shack to change into gym shorts, for it was now about a hundred degrees outside. Then we headed for the barn to pick up a lawnmower for my use. We lifted it onto the back of Dalton's Ford Pickup and then proceeded back to the boys' camp, where I was to start mowing. Dalton would cut the open areas with a tractor and bush-hog. With the lawnmower I was instructed to cut closely around the cabins and trees and anywhere else the tractor couldn't reach.

As I mentioned, the camp had two huge swimming pools. The boys' pool was set at the base of a fairly steep valley. The hotter it got, the longer I cut, the more my eyes kept straying to that cool blue rectangle. It wasn't filled completely, but almost so, mountain-cold water from the pipe still rushing out.

I'm pretty sure I was looking at the pool, when it happened. I was cutting the banks of a small dry creek that ran down the hill toward the pool. The small section the tractor couldn't get hadn't been cut all spring, so it was very high and thick. You had to let the blade slowly chew up the grass, or it would clog to a stop, so there was time to look around and not pay attention.

The first sting hit home on my lower left leg. I really felt that one—a sudden white-hot burning sensation. The second was on my other leg—and I felt that, too. After that I didn't feel any of them individually, just all together. When I looked down I saw my legs mostly covered with yellow/brown bees. Trying to knock them off, I slipped into the creek and briefly hit the ground, which didn't help any. They were all over me now—my neck, my back, my stomach.

When I bounced back up, I started running with no direction. Does a madman run in a direction? It was the closest thing to insanity I had ever experienced. My entire body was on fire. I didn't know it was possible to hurt so much all over at once. As I ran I could still feel them on me. I tried to knock them off my arms and stomach. I howled in pain—howled to high heaven.

I suppose it was natural that I should run downhill. The first thing I truly saw after the attack was the pool, and then I had a destination. Over the forty-yard distance I picked up speed, even after hitting the wide apron of the pool.

What I felt immersed in that ice-cold water wasn't exactly relief, but a whole lot better. I didn't know if any more bees were on me or not, so to make sure I brushed over the parts of my body I could reach. Already I could feel the welts. After that I put my head on the apron of the pool in exhaustion and just breathed with my eyes closed.

I heard a woman's voice: "Are you all right?"

When I looked up, I saw the sneakers and legs of two women standing there over me. "Bees," I said weakly. It was about all I could get out. Had it been a harder consonant to pronounce, I'm not sure I could have managed it. My head dropped back down.

They let me stay there a little while in the water, and then they fished me out, each taking a side under my armpits, first to a seated position on the apron with my legs in the water, and about ten seconds later they helped me to my feet. One of the women said she was a nurse, and they were taking me to the infirmary. I could walk, of course, though not very steadily. I think they each had a hand on my shoulder to start out our walk up the hill.

"What's your name?" the nurse asked me.

"Jacob... Jake."

"Jake what?"

"Jake Sullivan."

Inside the infirmary the nurse told me to take off my shirt. When I did, I saw five or six welts on my belly. My arms and legs were especially covered with them—big red welts. Not the nurse but the other woman, more a girl, took my shirt, and that was the last I saw of her. She went out the door. I recognized her, though I didn't say anything. I didn't know her, but I knew who she was; a guy I was acquainted with had taken her to the prom.

I sat down on a folding chair to remove my shoes and socks. "You want something to drink, don't you?" the nurse asked. I did, desperately. She gave me a choice between water and "bug juice." She explained it was Kool-Aid, but that was what they called it at Fort Ross. I opted for the bug juice.

She went to the refrigerator. "I'm Allie."

"It's nice to meet you, Allie."

"You're very polite," she said, "under the circumstances."

She put a red plastic cup on her desk and then poured from a plastic pitcher she had brought out of the refrigerator. I looked around. By the entry was her desk, and behind it was the fridge. I was sitting in an open area, where boxes were on the floor. Farther in were two beds on either side with bare mattresses. Toward the back was a black examination table. The walls were lined with glass cabinets, most empty.

I drained the first cup of bug juice while she was standing there. She brought another. "Why don't we get you on the examination table?" she said. "I've got some ointment somewhere."

"Let me just sit here for a minute, okay?"

"Okay."

I drank more bug juice. The first box she looked into, she found what she was looking for. She then proceeded farther away from me, out of the room. It was my first understanding that a small bedroom was back there. Music started to play.

When she came back out, she said. "It's terrible of me, I know. I set up my stereo first. I hope you like Bob Dylan."

Allie was about the most beautiful woman I had ever seen. Even down at the pool, as out of it as I was, I was aware of it. She had thick shoulder-length hair that was pulled back—a snow-white blonde. Her eyes were green, enormous. She had a soft rounded chin with just the slightest of a dimple. But what really made her face was her nose. It had a small upward slant that was nothing short of bewitching—just the most pleasing slope upward. She wasn't that tall—about five-three—but she curved in all the right places. She was a grown woman. I guessed her to be at least twenty-five.

"Are you ready now?" she asked.

I was. When I reached the examination table, I dropped down a bit harder onto it than I had expected to. The back of my head rested completely flat. "Man, did they get you," she said.

With a white cloth and some white ointment she started to dab the welts on my legs. The ointment did make them feel a little better. When she finished with my legs, I told her the ones on my neck hurt the most, so she went directly there. Her face was about six inches away from mine. She had the most flawless skin.

Bob Dylan wafted in the background. "The Times, They Are a-Changing" transitioned to "A Hard Rain's Gonna Fall."

"Do you like Dylan?" she asked me.

"He's okay. He's kind of hard to listen to."

"He's more than okay," Allie said. "He's probably the best poet this country has ever had. You want him to be able to sing, too?"

I rolled over on my stomach for the last of it. "I'm counting as we go," she said. "Do you want to know, or don't you?"

"I want to know."

"Forty-three," she said. As I rolled back over, she added, "It's a good thing you're not dead."

She brought me more bug juice. When she returned, I was sitting up on the examination table, dangling my legs. She handed me the red plastic cup and said, "You're not going anywhere for a while. Do you want me to make one of the beds?"

I didn't. I went back to the folding chair near her desk and placed my red plastic cup on it. Allie had one going there as well. She started to unpack boxes a few feet away from me. Seeing the side of her, I couldn't help but notice the pleasing swell of her bosom. I felt a little funny sitting here with just my gym shorts on. "What about my shirt?" I asked her.

"It's outside on the bench, drying in the sun," she responded. "I didn't want you to put it on yet, anyway. What are you studying in school? You're in college, right?"

I didn't get the feeling she was overly interested in me. Her question was akin to bedside manner. "History," I answered. "I won't be starting college until the fall. I'm thinking about becoming a lawyer, but I'm considering journalism, too."

She seemed to be listening but didn't venture an opinion on the subject. I took the opportunity to ask about her companion, if her name was Martha, and it was. Martha's father was a big-time attorney in town, almost famous.

"I just met her this morning," Allie said, taking a sip from her cup. "But I can tell you, she's a sweetheart."

Allie asked another generic question: "Do you like sports?"

"I love football," I said.

She sniffed her cute nose at it in favor of baseball. "Now *there's* an interesting game."

"Baseball's good," I said. "But there's nothing like football. At least for me, football is an intricate part of fall's seduction."

I don't know why I said that. I had never thought it before—it just kind of came out. I was embarrassed I had said it. She stopped unloading her box to look at me. Her head tilted a little to one side, and she studied me for a long second with a quizzical expression. I could feel my face turning red. "You ought to be a writer," she said finally, and with conviction.

"Maybe," I answered in a weak voice. I just wanted the moment over with.

"You're kind of a serious guy, aren't you? I mean, journalism, the law—that's serious business."

"Perhaps," I answered, and then tried my best to joke it off. "I'd flush them both down the toilet to play in the NFL."

She went back to her unpacking. "Could I use the restroom?" I asked.

"The bathroom is back off that room," she said, pointing toward the room where the music was coming from.

Her room was small. A gray suitcase rested on top of the bare mattress. Beside the bed was a night table with a lamp. On the wall opposite her bed was a dresser, upon which the stereo rested. There wasn't enough open space for even a chair. There was room enough, however, for a Bob Dylan poster, which was already hung at the head of her bed. Dylan's profile was silhouetted in black, while his flowing hair was a wild riot of color.

"I guess you like Bob Dylan," I said upon returning.

She laughed. "He's gone electric. I don't know about that. It's the difference in our age. Bob Dylan was as new and fresh to me as the Beatles were to you."

I sat in the same folding chair and reached for my red plastic cup. I took a sip and immediately spit it back into the cup. "What's *in* this?" I looked down at it. It appeared to be the same red bug juice I had been drinking.

"Oh, shit," she said, turning to me. "There's Vodka in there..." An awkward silence followed. She was embarrassed, and I was embarrassed for her. "I guess you could say I'm still celebrating," she said finally.

"Celebrating what?"

"About ten days ago, I got back from Vietnam."

"You were a nurse there?"

"Yes."

Another awkward pause. Of course, it was none of my business what she was doing drinking Kool-Aid and Vodka by herself at three o'clock in the afternoon, but the issue was kind of sitting there. I had the feeling I could have gone the whole summer without knowing she was in Vietnam, if not for a circumstance like this. "I'm still trying to get my land legs," she said.

"This seems like a good place to do it," I replied. I wanted to rescue her. "I hope I'm the worst case you have all summer. In a few weeks, you'll be right as rain."

"'Right as rain?' You say funny things."

She wasn't unpacking her boxes anymore. We were talking. The mishap with the cups had opened a small special door between us—or I was feeling that, and I believed maybe she was, too. "Can I ask you something?" I said. "Now that it's over, are you glad you went, or do you wish you had never gone?"

She didn't answer right away, but it wasn't as though she was formulating an answer. "I wish I had never gone over there."

"Thank you for telling me." I wasn't about to ask any more.

"Life is cheap," she added, and I was happy to listen. "I learned there are parts of this world where life is as cheap as a single dollar." I stayed still and let her ruminate. "The worst is telling a twenty-year-old kid who's all shot up that he still has a future. It makes you feel old. Some days I felt as old as the hills. I still do."

"You're not old. You're tired... How old are you?"

"Twenty-six. How old are you?"

"Nineteen."

It was then that Dalton pulled up to the infirmary on his tractor. I heard it first and then saw him through the window. His timing was pretty poor, as far as I was concerned. Allie and I were just starting to talk, and I wanted more of it.

When he came through the screen door, he had my shirt. I supposed it was how he knew I was in here. He noticed Allie most definitely, but he was diplomatic enough to turn his attention almost immediately to me. "What happened to you?" he asked, laughing.

I started to tell him, and he cut me off. "I know what happened to you. I saw where the lawnmower is." Again, he just laughed with his blue eyes twinkling.

"It's not funny," Allie said.

Dalton didn't even attempt to appease her. "Yeah, it is. I mean, come on, look at him. It looks like someone used him for a dartboard."

"Glad you're enjoying it," I said. Even I was beginning to appreciate the humor of it.

Allie still didn't see it that way. "He could have died. He got stung forty-three times."

When Dalton heard the number, he just about bent over in laughter. He clapped his hands together. I started laughing, too. Allie didn't like it. I think she muttered, "Morons," under her breath.

Dalton said I was having a bang-up day. We told Allie how we had spent our morning, with Dalton finding no reason to spare details. Dalton could fill up a room when he wanted to—and he wanted to. It was all for Allie, and I think she knew it. "You about ready for another cigarette, Jake?" Dalton asked.

Allie looked to me. "Do you smoke?"

"No." I laughed. "Not 'til today."

Allie turned to Dalton. "Don't be giving him cigarettes."

"You're right," Dalton said respectfully. "When you're right, you're right." He tossed me my T-shirt. "We'll get some gasoline at the barn. Those bees aren't going to know what hit them."

Allie objected immediately, as I was pulling on my shirt. "He's not going anywhere near that nest."

I liked it that she was protective of me. Not for the first time, I felt a small bond between us, more than simply patient and nurse. I wished I could have continued talking to her in the mood we were in, but Dalton had changed that.

"Can I go now?" I asked her. "I'm feeling better."

"To go blow up that nest?" she asked.

"Yeah. To go blow up that nest."

She shook her head with resignation. "All right. You boys go out and play."

Allie stepped outside with us while I sat on the bench and put on my socks and shoes. Allie asked Dalton if she could have some white paint to spruce up the bench. It was a neat old bench, at least ten feet long with a high back and ornate arms and legs. Dalton said yes, and Allie went inside. I was glad for that. When I finished tying my sneakers, I went back inside the infirmary.

"I just wanted to thank you," I said to Allie.

She gave me a nice smile. "You're welcome. You're my first patient."

"I hope you have a good summer here. It sounds like you deserve it."

"Thank you," she said with a soft voice. As I was turning to leave, she added, "I'm glad you didn't get any stings on your face. That would have been a shame."

As I stood behind Dalton on the tractor ride back to the barn, he had one subject on his mind: Allie. Who was she? What did I know about her? I didn't say from where she had recently returned. I figured it was her business to tell people that. I just said she was really nice. Dalton went on about how attractive she was. I didn't add to it.

"I want to paint that bench for her," I said when we reached the barn.

Dalton chuckled. "Jake, she's out of your league, buddy." Then he really started laughing. "She's Mt. Everest, and you're wearing flip-flops."

I knew I had no chance with her, but I still wanted to do it. I liked her a lot, and I wanted to do something nice for her.

Dalton and I grabbed a metal bucket and a full gasoline can from the barn. When we pulled up in Dalton's blue Ford to my abandoned lawnmower, I started to shake a little. It all came back to me in a rush. One welt on my neck was particularly bad and started throbbing more at the sight of the crime.

First Dalton dragged the lawnmower away from the nest. Then, on the bed of the pick-up, he poured five or six inches of gasoline into the bottom of the bucket. It was a lot of gasoline. I had a book of matches. From about twenty yards Dalton ran at the nest first. I struck the book of matches and followed. By the time I reached the hole, Dalton had dumped the gasoline on the nest. Right after I tossed the book of matches toward it. I was on the run, so I didn't see it, but I felt the explosion. It was very loud.

Dalton and I stood together, watching the white smoke rise. Allie came out of the screen door of the infirmary, looking in our direction.

* * * * *

The next day at about four o'clock I went back to the infirmary with a can of white paint and a brush. As I approached, I could hear Bob Dylan playing. Allie stepped out and asked me how my stings were doing. She looked even more beautiful. All night and day I had thought about her, how pretty she was. My memory couldn't do her justice. She was twice as pretty today.

She reached for the paint can, and I drew it back from her. "I'm going to do it for you," I said.

"Jake, I'll do it. I've got time."

"I want to do it. To thank you."

"Okay," she said. "Have at it. Do you want me to help?"

"No. I want to do it for you. I only brought one brush."

"I guess that settles that. I'll be inside, if you need anything."

As she was going back in, I said, "Hey, why don't you turn up Dylan for me?"

She cranked it.

I was there for about forty-five minutes, and she never came back out. When I was finished, I headed for the barn without letting her know. I really didn't want her to thank me, and I didn't want to make a nuisance of myself by hanging around. I didn't want to benefit from it in any way.

Chapter Two

On Friday at six o'clock I ceased being a temporary member of the maintenance department. The entire staff arrived in anticipation of the camp opening Sunday at noon. Saturday was orientation for new and old staff alike, with a lot of sitting around and listening in the boys' mess hall. Bernie was director of the boys' camp; Sister Helen headed the girls' camp. While they did almost all the talking, I kept a keen eye on the comings and goings of the maintenance trucks, wishing I were out with Dalton, Stevie and Uncle Bob.

That Friday evening, the first thing we did was to celebrate Mass in the red brick chapel. There were about a hundred of us: fifty college-aged guys and fifty college-aged girls. Father White, the presiding director of Fort Ross, was in his forties—a pale, mousy little man with a voice that was hardly forceful or endearing. His sermon was bland. He didn't strike me as someone who should be running a summer camp.

Bernie, however, easily made up for Father White's lack of personality. Bernie was the person I interviewed with. He was a big, enthusiastic man with a beer-belly and a deep voice that could be heard counties away. He taught at a Catholic high school during the year and was head basketball coach for a usually successful team. A couple of years his team nearly advanced to the end of the state championship.

Sister Helen wore T-shirts and shorts like everyone else, but you still sort of knew she was a nun. She moved kind of hesitantly around. She was in her forties, too, I think—but with her it was somewhat hard to tell, for she had an ageless quality. There was a benevolence about her, too. The veteran girl counselors ran circles around her, because she just couldn't believe any of them would do anything wrong. Bernie wasn't stupid.

A veteran counselor was customarily paired with a rookie for the first of the camp's five two-week periods. My veteran counselor was Stuart. I'm certain Dalton had a hand in the pairing; he and Stuart were good friends and had been together three summers here. Stuart was laid-back, his brown hair was a little longer than the of the rest of us, and he was filled-out with a heavy beard on a plain round face—quite the contrast to the thinness of Dalton and me.

"She is going make me pay," Stuart said. "I mean, she is going to make me *pay!*"

It was Saturday night about ten o'clock. Dalton and I were sitting on empty bunks in Stuart's cabin while he was changing clothes for the evening. "When was the last time you talked to her?" Dalton asked him.

"Christmas," Stuart said. "All I've gotten from her so far is the stink-eye."

"There are a lot of fish in the sea. We got a fresh new crop."

In a few minutes' time, we would be heading for the boys' shack. It was the only building that was actually built in the woods, about seventy-five yards into the forest, accessed by a road just wide enough to fit a vehicle. About ten o'clock every Tuesday and Thursday nights the girls came up to mix with the boys and drink beer in the basement of the boys' shack.

"Tonight is opening night," Dalton said. "You'd better pick one, Jake, before all the good ones are gone."

The basement entrance was around the back of the shack as you approached it. To enter, you had to go down a concrete ramp with knee-walls that were good for sitting on. The Rolling Stones were rocking out the first time I started down the ramp, behind Dalton and Stuart.

The basement was a drab, dark place with concrete walls and floors. The floors were always damp. Christmas lights strung on three walls brightened it a little. Just to the right as you stepped inside was a stand-up bar run by two enterprising counselors who marked you down for a quarter a beer on the list they had. It came out of your money on payday. If not nice, it was a big space, maybe thirty yards long. It had a picnic table and two regular tables with chairs, and against one wall was a long shuffleboard table that was never played on, only sat upon. The basement's back end was for the water-heater and dancing; the music came from there, and it was darkest back there. From the stand-up bar at the entrance there was descending light.

We were fashionably late, so the mixer was in full swing. Right away Dalton and Stuart got snagged by some of their old friends. I continued on. Thumper, a drinking game, was underway at one of the tables, with about ten participants pounding on the edge of the table with their open hands.

I looked for Martha and saw her sitting on top of the picnic table with another girl. Martha and I had twice exchanged friendly smiles, once at the chapel and once while filing out of the boys' mess hall, but we hadn't spoken since she helped Allie fish me from the pool. I placed myself before them with more ease than usual, because I had something to say: "I just wanted to thank you properly for helping me."

"Oh, you're welcome," Martha replied sweetly. "I didn't do anything."

She was very pretty in a refined sort of way. She had big brown eyes and a small, straight nose. Her thick auburn hair was cut neatly at her shoulders. Perhaps it was the way her hair was cut that gave you the idea she was from money—not just money, but old money. It applied for most of us, but more so for Martha, that she had lived her entire life in a cocoon of wealth.

"This is C.C.," Martha said, motioning to her colleague. "She's my buddy counselor to start out with."

I tried not to smile, and I don't think I did. C.C. was the name of Stuart's girlfriend from last summer. She was pretty, too, but in a very different way: she was earthy, with long brown hair and a stout figure. She looked me straight in the eye. Right away I started feeling sorry for Stuart. There was something about C.C. that was strong.

I was asking C.C. how many summers she had worked at Fort Ross, when Allie appeared and sat on the picnic table with them. She handed C.C. a can of beer. Allie's blonde hair was always pulled back before, so this was the first time I had seen it down. It fell gloriously down a couple inches below her neck and somehow made that gentle slope of her nose even more pleasing. She had on a sleeveless white linen blouse that shaped her figure. Most of the girls were in blouses. The guys wore mainly T-shirts, but their better ones.

After C.C. answered my question, Allie asked, "How's my first patient?"

"Fine," I answered. The sight of her looking like this had knocked me off-kilter. I wanted to add more but couldn't.

Then Dalton presented himself. "Look at Jake, hogging all the pretty girls." He took the spot standing next to me. "C.C., I don't know how you do it. Every year you get more beautiful."

She just smiled at him at first—a knowing smile. "Where's your side-kick?"

"Am I my brother's keeper? He'll turn up. He has to."

Of course, I knew the background for this conversation. It seemed to me that Martha and Allie did, too. I was standing across from C.C. A floor-to-ceiling support column was next to us. Martha was seated in the middle, and Allie was farthest from me.

Next, Dalton turned to Allie. "And good evening to the medical department."

Allie merely nodded, because it was obvious Dalton was angling for an introduction to the third person who was seated in the middle. I didn't feel it was my place to do it—I felt it was C.C.'s.

"I'm not introducing you to her, Dalton," C.C. said. "I don't want that on my ledger."

Martha's brown eyes opened a little wider, and you could tell she was interested and enjoying the attention. She stuck out her hand. "I'm Martha."

As Dalton was taking it, C.C. said, "Dalton, why don't you pick on someone your own age?"

Dalton turned to C.C. "I'm not picking on her. I just want to talk to her, maybe ask her to dance." Then he turned to Martha. "I think what we have here is a transference of hostility. She doesn't really mean it."

"I don't know," Martha replied with a playfulness in her voice. "I'm supposed to listen to her. If C.C. is telling me something, I should probably trust it."

Dalton heaved a heavy sigh. "She can't say one bad thing about me," he said to Martha, and then turned back to C.C. "You can't, C.C. We've spent three summers here. You, me and Stuart, last summer, we ran all over this place together, and never have we ever had a cross word. I dare you. Say something bad about me. I'm too nice? I'm too optimistic. I'm too—"

"You talk too much."

Dalton turned triumphantly to Martha. "I rest my case."

Stuart chose this moment to sidle up next to Dalton. How we were situated couldn't have been worse for him. With the support column where it was, if he wanted to talk to C.C., he would have to do so diagonally across the six of us.

"Hi," he said weakly to C.C.

"How are you, Stuart? You're looking well."

"Oh, man, this is worse than I thought," Dalton said. "She's going to be *nice?*"

"Shut up, Dalton," C.C. said, still looking at Stuart.

"Can we talk alone?" Stuart asked her.

"What's wrong with here?"

We four observers were now required for this public humiliation. Not that I wanted to go anywhere—I was dying to hear it out. Martha was, too. Her eyes were wide with interest, and she was leaning a little forward. Allie was taking it in with not much expression, but she was absolutely paying attention.

"Well," C.C. asked, "what do you have to say for yourself?"

"I apologize," Stuart said. "You could have called me too. I meant to call you. And then the longer it got, I knew you'd be mad."

"So you just let me get madder?"

"That wasn't the plan."

Dalton's heart was in the right place. "Come on, guys. It's just a little misunderstanding. Stuart was wrong, and he's sorry."

"You're not walking me home tonight," C.C. said to Stuart. "You can forget about that."

Then there was a pause, which Dalton seized. He asked Martha if she wanted to dance. She did, and they headed toward the back of the basement. C.C. removed herself from the picnic table and headed in the opposite direction. Stuart followed her, leaving me alone with Allie.

"This is like Peyton Place," I said to her with a smile.

"She won't last very long," Allie said. "She likes him."

"Can I join you?"

"Of course."

I sat on top of the picnic table next to her. I was quite happy to have her alone—the most beautiful woman in the room, the most beautiful woman anywhere. There may have been a hundred other people in the basement, but, as far as I was concerned, there was only one now.

"Thanks for painting my bench," she said. "It looks really nice. Why didn't you tell me when you were finished? I looked out, and you were gone."

"I didn't want to bother you. I didn't paint the bench because I wanted to hang out. I guess I was afraid you might think that."

"I get it," she said. "You're sweet."

We sat and talked for a long time. She said her younger sister was getting married at the end of the summer, and that was the reason she had taken this job: to be around for the wedding and also use the time to apply to hospitals, one in California she was particularly interested in. It came out that both of our fathers were doctors, general practitioners. She asked me if I ever considered medicine as a career.

"One of my brothers is in medical school," I answered, "but not me. I found out in freshman biology that I don't like squishy things. That was when I started thinking about becoming a lawyer. At least the law is clean and dry, and nobody calls you in the middle of the night."

We talked about our families. Allie said her little sister had been fired from her job as a lay teacher because of her impending nuptials. Either she was going to get pregnant, which the priest didn't want, or she would use birth control to prevent pregnancy. Either way, when she announced her engagement, the parish priest called her in, and she found out she was no longer worthy of employment by the Catholic Church.

"You don't have to keep sitting here with me," Allie said. "I know it's kind of an important evening for you guys."

"I like talking to you," I said, and I meant it.

"You haven't seen a girl you're interested in?"

I gave a small laugh. "Well, Martha... I had noticed her."

"Oh," Allie said. "Sorry."

"I'm pretty shy with girls."

"That's all right," Allie said with a soft, sympathetic voice. "It's better to be shy than too much the other way. Lots of good girls like shy."

Again, I felt it with her—a kind of special bond. She liked me, I could tell, and I knew I liked her. Of course, she didn't feel the same way about me that I did toward her: to her I was a little brother and she was my confidant. At least for now, I was willing to take what she was offering. I was grateful for it. In fact, I was ecstatic over it.

I thought about asking her how she was doing in getting her land legs, but I didn't. Something told me not to, and what she said next made me glad I didn't, for she was ready to bolt. "I've made my appearance," she said. "You guys can carry on without me."

I knew what she was saying—that she wasn't truly a part of us. "I'm glad you came."

"Me too." She gave me a kind, warm smile as she stood. "You didn't say anything funny tonight. Work on that."

As she was turning away from me, I called after her. "Hey. What's your last name?"

"Smith." Her shoulders moved in a slight shrug.

Sitting there, I watched her all the way to the door. I wished I were walking her home. Of course, it was ridiculous, but that was what I was thinking—that I belonged more by her side walking her home right now than I didn't. After just a couple of meetings, a special relationship was growing between us. Not for the first time, I thought back to the day I was leaving the infirmary, when she said it would have been a shame if I had gotten any stings on my face. I was going out the screen door with my back to her when she had said it.

Was she trying to tell me she thought I had an attractive face?

The rest of the night I spent mostly with Stuart and some of the other new boy counselors. I didn't meet anyone special from the other side. Dalton was never far away from Martha, though most of the time he didn't have her exclusively. C.C. was hanging around. The private conversation she had with Stuart must have been short.

At the end of the night, I was standing near the door with Dalton, Martha and Stuart when C.C. joined us. "Are you ready to go?" she asked Martha.

"Come on, C.C." Dalton said in protest. "You're killing me."

Martha laughed, enjoying this. "It's nice to be wanted."

"You can blame Stuart that I need someone to walk me home."

"There's probably five girls still here that are all going down together," Dalton said.

"Good night, *boys*."

Once they were gone, the three of us sat on the concrete wall outside and finished our beers. "This is not good, guys," Dalton said. "This is *not* good."

* * * * *

Incoming Sunday, as it was called, was a flurry of activity. In a four-hour span, over four hundred kids with parents and grandparents and siblings arrived. Just about every kid came with an inexpensive steamer trunk. The steamer trunks were unloaded in a field just inside the main gate and transported in a big cattle truck up to the camps. There was always something very hopeful about Incoming Sunday. Bright, cheery music played over the loudspeakers in each camp, including Allan

Sherman's "Hello Muddah, Hello Faddah." A mounted Indian and a cowboy dressed to the nines trotted around together and separately. The cowboy's mare had a red foal that stayed very close, so it was a double hit.

As I mentioned, if you went straight up the hill from the entrance, you ended up at the barn and the farm and Charlie's house. About halfway up that hill you made a right turn at Father White's house to get to the camps. Once you made that turn, you went more or less straight to get to the girls' camp. For the boys' camp, you made a left turn to go farther up the hill. From the front gate to the back woods was one big climb upward, though there were many hills within the hills. Perhaps it was a fifteen-minute walk from the gate to where the woods started behind the boys' camp.

The camps were set up almost exactly the same. Each had eighteen white cabins that formed an upside-down 'V' on a gently sloping hill. At the point of the 'V' was the 'nine-and-a-half,' a big building with shower and toilet facilities. In the middle of the 'V,' a flagpole sprang from a five-foot-square concrete base perfect for sitting on. The flagpole's base was a hub for each camp, where Bernie and Sister Helen could stand and address the campers in person instead of over the loudspeaker. Reveille and Taps were played each day over the loudspeaker, with everyone lined up and saluting.

Father White dressed in black and his collar only on Incoming Sunday. Everyone else looked pretty much the same, except for Allie. When I first saw her, I was in the playhouse, another very big building. It had an indoor basketball court and wings for the nature department's displays and instruction. My job that Incoming Sunday was, along with others, to take every camper's temperature. The infirmary was the next building down, about twenty-five yards. Technically the infirmary was between the two camps, but truly it was the last, lowest building of the boys' camp.

When Allie entered the playhouse for the first time, she was a vision in white. I almost dropped my clipboard when I saw her in her white uniform and white stockings. I was transfixed. There was a bright white aura about her, as if she were floating around in a halo instead of walking. I couldn't take my eyes off that soothing white glow as it hovered from place to place.

Maybe four times she came into the playhouse that afternoon, and every time I felt the same. She was the most beautiful woman I had ever seen, and now it was taking on saintly proportions. Was I starting to go crazy over her? I think I was. And what red-blooded guy wouldn't?

Stuart and I had Cabins 7 and 8, respectively, which meant our boys were ten years old. We met them about four in the afternoon. They were good, fun kids. Eight of my nine boys were from the same Catholic grade school; the ninth was Timmy Campbell. For his second summer in a row, Timmy would spend all of it at Fort Ross, as his parents traveled Europe in the summer. He seemed to be a good-natured kid, somewhat quiet. He was a little smaller than average, with brown hair and a delicate face.

The maintenance department had nothing to do with the campers, but Dalton made an exception for Timmy. Four or five times a week he picked up Timmy in his battered blue Ford and drove him to the mess halls, where they gathered up garbage cans full of slop for Charlie's pigs. Barely an ounce of food was wasted at

Fort Ross. Campers dumped even the smallest leftover into a steel can before turning in their plates. By the end of the day each mess hall had two full cans, usually. They varied in weight depending on the fare, but Timmy insisted on helping Dalton load them onto the bed of the truck no matter how heavy they were. Probably the whole thing took fifteen minutes, but Timmy loved doing it. "I'm king of the pigs," he said to me, and I knew exactly what he meant by it. Dalton let Timmy hold up his arm to quiet the pigs down.

Each day at eight o'clock, both camps lined up for Reveille at the flagpole, and then headed for the mess hall. After breakfast was cabin cleanup and inspection, for which first, second and third place banners were awarded and hung on the award-winning cabins for the day. At nine-thirty the daily programs began: the kids would go to riding, swimming, handicraft, or nature. Sometimes the kids wouldn't have a program to go to, and the counselors were on duty.

On Monday, the first full day of camp, rain came down in buckets. On rainy days there was no swimming or riding. Alternative programs existed, however. One was something called a 'mud hike.' I didn't completely understand it when I volunteered. I thought we were just going to walk around the woods in the rain. I had about twenty kids of all ages with me, including maybe four of my campers. The second we entered the woods, where the trail was wide enough for a car, three veteran campers shot by me on the run and then belly-flopped straight down into the mud, sliding about ten feet. That was when I really understood what 'mud hike' meant.

There were some particularly good spots in the girls' part of the woods, which we eventually approached.

"Wait 'til we get to the next one," a camper said to me. I admit I was impressed when I saw it. For about fifty feet, water was rushing down this one muddy hill like a log flume. I couldn't resist. By now I had so much mud on me anyway, from the kids splashing around me. I think I went down it four times, and to hearty cheers from the campers every time. It was fun.

We came out of the woods in the girls' camp, which meant we had to walk by the infirmary to get to the boys' camp. I was bringing up the rear with stragglers. Allie popped her head out of the screen door to view the passage of brown blobs in a single-file line. She didn't see me at first. When she did, she smiled and said, "You goof!"

That was the only time I saw her all week, other than the three times daily in the mess hall, which really didn't count. Allie didn't come to the Tuesday night mixer, nor the Thursday one. Dalton walked Martha home on both occasions. C.C. and Stuart, however, were still on the outs.

By Friday, Dalton had a plan to get them together, which included me recruiting Allie. Dalton wanted to get together a fairly big group for a campfire in the woods, a group big enough so C.C. would come, for Allie, Martha and C.C. had been spending time together. If I could get Allie to come, C.C. probably would, too.

Allie had a morning call during cabin cleanup and an evening call after dinner, so I knocked on the infirmary's screen door at about eight-thirty, when I was sure her last duties were done. Dylan was playing softly. She welcomed me in with a nice smile. Inside looked a lot different than the last time I had seen it. There weren't any boxes anywhere. The two beds were made. The glass cabinets on the walls were filled. Camper artwork was stuck to the refrigerator behind her desk. She kept her desk mostly clear, except for a couple of writing tablets and a blotter.

"Sit down," she said. I took the folding chair by her desk. "Do you want some watermelon?"

"Sure." I appreciated the offer. I got the feeling she was glad to see me—or, at the very least, she didn't mind my visit.

Allie opened her fridge and pulled out half a watermelon. She sliced a piece on her desk and then put it on a plate for me. "Dalton wanted me to ask you something," I said.

"Why doesn't he do it himself?" Allie asked. "He's in here every day, supposedly to pick up my garbage. He pours himself bug juice and starts talking."

I told Allie the plan, how her presence would be greatly appreciated.

"Sure," Allie said. "I'll come, as long as I don't have a camper that needs to stay overnight."

"Good." I was now looking forward to it more than anyone.

"I know why Dalton didn't ask me. He knew I wouldn't say no to you."

I was surprised she said that, and very pleased. It wasn't all in my head—there *was* a small special bond between us, and she was acknowledging it, acknowledging that even others recognized it. With that I felt confident enough to ask her, "How are you doing? Are you feeling a little better now?"

"Are you worried about me? I'm doing okay. If the first week is any gauge, I'll be well rested by the end of the summer."

"Can I ask you something? You're not coming to the mixers anymore?"

"We'll see," she answered. "Probably I will."

* * * * *

The following night, the night of the campfire, Stuart and I had cabin-walk together. It was a nice warm evening. Cabin-walk was from nine to eleven. Evening programs ended at nine, and the counselors were free from then until eleven, when they were supposed to be in bed. Cabin-walk meant covering that two-hour period. Mostly it meant sitting on the base of the flagpole and occasionally walking over to a cabin, not yet ready to give it up for the night.

"I bet she doesn't even come," Stuart said.

What I was thinking about was Allie. I was hoping every camper was feeling just fine.

We had a long walk to the campfire. Dalton's favorite spot in the woods was beyond the farm side of the property, far away from where any campers would be sleeping out the night. We went by the barn and the pigs, who were sleeping, I supposed. Then we walked along the fence line of a cow pasture before reaching the woods. Luckily, we didn't need to go that far in.

We heard music playing as we approached, and then we saw the campfire light. We stepped into a nice, flat open area. C.C. and Allie were both there, sitting next to each other on a tree trunk with Martha.

"Boys!" Dalton said, in greeting us.

Pleasantries were exchanged. Stuart said hello to C.C., and she didn't spit in his face. I was so glad to see Allie, and I think she was glad to see me. She gave me a nice smile. Tree trunks for sitting on surrounded three of the four sides of the fire. One was unoccupied, which Stuart and I took. Stevie and Uncle Bob were seated on the trunk across from us. The girls were to my right. Dalton was standing in the open area with a big white cooler at his leather boots.

If there might have been some awkwardness with Stuart joining C.C., Dalton took care of it. He drew out a couple of cans from the cooler for Stuart and me, and then he started talking. "Beer has to be cold. I mean *cold!* There's nothing worse than drinking warm beer in the woods, like they used to do here when I started. *Heathens!*" Then he did about a minute on the right amount of ice in the cooler per can. He had to figure in the hot dogs. That cost at least a beer.

"Dalton," Martha said in a playful voice, "why does that cooler say 'Father White' on the side of it?"

"Merely borrowed, I assure you, Martha. I'll take it back."

"Father White seems like a weird guy, doesn't he?" Stuart said. "He just kind of lurks around."

"He smells," C.C. said. "The other day I was using his car to take something up to the boys' camp. About half the way, I drove with my head out the window."

"I don't think he's that bad of a guy," Dalton said. "He's just a little socially awkward. He doesn't know how to talk to people."

"He doesn't say much in the mess hall," Allie remarked. "But no one can say too much with Bernie at the table."

Allie was wearing her hair down again, the first time I had seen it since the opening mixer. She had on crisp khaki shorts. I tried not to look at her legs too much. I tried not to look at her too much in general. If I could get away with it, I would have stared at that gentle slope of her nose all night.

White smoke from the fire started wafting directly at my face, so I moved to the other side of the fire to sit with Stevie and Uncle Bob. Dalton told Allie and Martha that they lived nearby and worked for Charlie during the winter between going to school.

"We're the hillbillies of the group," Stevie said with a proud smile. "And we've got the John Deere hats to prove it."

"Don't say that," Martha replied sweetly. "You're in college like everyone else."

"He means they didn't go to private Catholic schools," Dalton volunteered.

"We went to school with girls," Stevie said. "And thank God we did."

"Craziest thing I ever heard of," said Uncle Bob.

It was true that the rest of us attended same-sex private Catholic high schools. Even Allie said she had; she was cut from the exact same cloth. The high schools socialized with each other. It was how I knew Martha's face, who she was. Dalton and I had attended the same Jesuit high school, though three years apart. We talked a little while about the pluses and minuses of same-sex schools. Martha said she had never really even thought about it.

The smoke attacked me again, so I resumed my original spot. Dalton passed out another round from his precious cooler. I got the feeling there was a time limit on this. We had only so much beer, and there were eight of us.

I took about two sips of my fresh beer, and the smoke was on me again. It was just uncanny, like I was a magnet. Everyone enjoyed it, including Allie. "Jake, sit with the girls," Dalton said. "Let's see if it gets you there."

I had to get up, so I did, next to Martha. "Who's going to sit with him when we're eating?" Dalton asked.

"I will," Allie said. "The poor guy."

To cook the hot dogs, we needed sticks for skewers. Dalton and Martha went in one direction looking, Allie and I in another. "I'm glad you came," I said.

"Me too," she replied. "I love campfires. I just love fires in general."

Allie and I skewered our hot dogs together. She held the sticks while I stuck them on. Dalton told Martha that a little bit of tree bark was good for her. Martha wasn't so sure.

All of us at once started cooking around the fire. Dalton and C.C. were bent over it next to each other. "C.C., quit touching my wiener," Dalton said. "Stuart, she's touching my wiener."

We all laughed.

"I am *not*," C.C. said. "You're touching *my* wiener."

"How can I be touching your wiener, when you don't have one?"

Allie was laughing hard. Her whole face lit with it. In the firelight her skin had this golden glow. I had never seen her like this. I had never seen any woman so beautiful.

Dalton wasn't ready to let go of it. "Stuart, she's doing it again. She's playing with my wiener." Finally, C.C. removed herself. She went to the other side of the fire and took a spot next to Stuart. I really don't think that was Dalton's plan, but it worked out that way.

Stuart and C.C. sat next to each other while we ate. Allie sat with me. "This is about the best hot dog I ever had," Allie said to Dalton. "Are these special?"

"No," Dalton answered. "I got the hot dogs and buns from Lil."

After we ate, Dalton handed out another round of beer. "This is the last of it. Guys, save your pee for putting out the fire. You girls feel free to do anything you want with your bladders."

Without saying anything, Stuart lit a joint and then passed it to C.C. Right away, he lit another. "This is all time-tested," Dalton said to no one in particular. "First you drink a little, then you eat, then you smoke."

I had smoked weed a few times before, but Martha hadn't. When the joint came to her, she held it in her hand, looking down. "Just pass it on, if you don't want it," C.C. said quietly. That was what she did the first time, but not when it came again. She coughed on her first drag, and the second one, too. Allie didn't cough. I could tell this wasn't her first rodeo.

Martha was first to show the effects of an altered mind. "Stevie, Uncle Bob, let me ask you something. Are you guys Catholic?"

Stevie said he was Lutheran. Uncle Bob said he was a Methodist.

"*Good*," Martha said. "I was just thinking to myself: I don't know one person who's not Catholic. I mean, I don't know *anybody* who's not Catholic. Isn't that ridiculous? You know what? I don't think my mother does, either. I don't think she knows anyone who's not Catholic."

"You're not the only one like that," C.C. said.

"What do you expect, Martha?" Dalton said. "Your old man's big with the church. Doesn't he know the archbishop?"

"Still," Martha said, "I should know somebody." She added brightly, "Well, now I know Stevie and Uncle Bob."

For some reason, Dalton started talking about the history of Fort Ross, none of which I knew. The camp opened in 1921. The whole shooting match was donated by one family in memory of a lost son, a Doughboy in the Great War. His body wasn't recovered. Members of the family viewed this property as sacred ground, kind of an alternative cemetery, that's what Charlie said. Charlie had taken over as caretaker in the late Twenties.

We didn't sit there that much longer—maybe twenty minutes—before the beer was gone and Dalton was ready to move on. He wanted to be alone with Martha, no doubt, as it was time to see what would happen between Stuart and C.C. The fire had burned pretty far down. Dalton dumped mostly water and a little ice from the cooler onto it, causing a great rush of white smoke. "All right, girls," Dalton announced, "It's show-time." The five of us finished it off.

Without the fire, it seemed very dark as we started for the trail. Stuart and C.C. carried the white cooler between them, each with a side handle. We threw the empty cans into the cooler, so it clanked a little as they walked. I thought it was a good sign. Allie did, too. She nudged me in the side and pointed at them ahead of us.

We were all still buzzed, so it wasn't that easy walking on the trails in the woods. When we hit the clearing, however, the sky was lit with stars as brightly as I had ever seen. It was a country sky, wide and open, the kind you never see in the city. We all stopped just at the clearing. "Oh, wow," Martha said in THC-induced wonderment. We stood there for a while, taking it in. With the full moon, the panorama was more blue than black. I had never seen so many different colors of stars—blue, yellow, green, orange—varying so dramatically in brightness.

On the trails in the woods, we had spread out some, but now we were moving forward again in a tight group. We proceeded along the fence line of the cow pasture. Stevie said the fence was newly electrified, due to Charlie's failing health. He said it for my benefit and Stuart's. No campers were supposed to be on the farm, but sometimes the boys came out of the woods here.

"Would it kill you?" Martha asked.

"No, no," Stevie said. "Farmers don't want to kill their cows. It would give you a jolt, though."

We walked about ten more steps, and I heard Stuart say, "Hey, Dalton."

"What?"

"I dare you to touch that fence."

Stevie and Uncle Bob started laughing immediately, because they knew Dalton. I joined them, because I knew him, too, enough.

"I'll touch it if you touch it," Dalton answered.

We stopped walking. Dalton and Stuart got into a discussion about who was going to go first. Stevie settled it right quick. "You can do it at the same time. All you have to do is hold hands. It'll go through both of you."

"Nooooo," Dalton said. "Really?"

"I think he knows what he's talking about," Stuart said. "He's studying to become an electrical engineer."

"Would it go through all eight of us, if we held hands?"

"Yeah."

"Oh, *man!*"

"There's no way, Dalton," C.C. said, laughing.

"Come on! We're all so stoned right now, nobody's going to feel a thing."

"We'll feel it," Stevie said.

Of course, there was no way Dalton was letting this thing go. In retrospect, as soon as we stopped walking, we were doomed. Dalton turned to Allie first. "You're in, right?"

Allie took a moment. "Yeah, I'm in."

"The nurse is in," Dalton said, triumphant. "It's practically approved by the AMA."

Allie was a good place to start. Once he had her, there was no stopping him. Stevie and Uncle Bob folded like cheap suits. If Allie was in, I was. Martha took a bit of work. You could tell she really wanted to do it for Dalton, yet she didn't really want to do it. I never doubted he would persuade her. C.C. was the last holdout. It took him five minutes, but eventually he got even her.

Dalton insisted on being the one to do the touching, which C.C. howled about. "I don't want to be on the end! God knows what happens on the end after eight people."

"Nothing more should happen," Stevie said.

"*You* get on the end, then!" C.C. told him.

We lined up in the grassy field with Dalton closest to the fence, of course, then Martha. I held hands with Martha and Allie. Stuart and C.C. were next. Uncle Bob and Stevie rounded out the back end. When I held Allie's hand, she looked at me, and we gave each other big smiles under the moonlight. She wasn't an adult, the responsible nurse—she was just one of us tonight.

"The first time I'm barely going to touch it," Dalton said. "That one doesn't count."

"We'll see about that," C.C. replied.

"All right, I'm going to count it down from three. Three. Two. One."

We were all braced for it, and Dalton started laughing. "Dalton!" C.C. said. The rest of us started laughing, too.

"All right, all right. Here we go... Three. Two. One."

This time Dalton touched it. I was watching him now. There wasn't an arc when he touched it or any sound, but I felt it. All of us felt it at once, a sudden current passing through us. It wasn't overwhelming, but it was strong enough to cause my shoulders to shudder. As quickly as it came, it was over. We all started laughing. When I looked to Allie, she squeezed my hand.

"That's it for me," C.C. said.

"Come on, C.C," Dalton said.

"No, Dalton. I know you're going to grab it this time."

Of course, there was nothing he could say to convince her otherwise. We were all still holding hands, so Dalton just grabbed it. The shock of it—and I do mean shock—had a little to do with the fact that we weren't expecting it, and just about everything with the amount of contact he made. I felt the current all the way down to my toes. The duration seemed like an eternity compared to the first round of voltage.

I don't think anyone was knocked to the ground, but we were holding hands and just kind of fell to the ground together when it finally stopped. We were all laughing and rolling around in the grass. I didn't think any of us wanted any more of it, but Martha proved me wrong. "I think I just peed in my pants," she said, giggling. "Let's do it again."

We didn't. But it was a little bit of time before we moved. We sat in the grass for a while and just looked up at the stars, at the glorious blue sky, at the huge orange moon. For once, even Dalton didn't have anything to say, at least for a while.

"Hey, Stevie, how far would it go? Let's say we got everyone in the world holding hands, and I touch that fence. How far would it go?"

"I don't know... I think you took one too many hits on that joint."

"Well, ask your professor that when you get back to school."

"Sure, Dalton. I'll tell him all about tonight. I'm trying to graduate one day."

When we began again, Dalton and Martha took Father White's cooler. Stuart and C.C. held hands for the last one hundred yards to the barn, where we separated upon reaching Stevie and Uncle Bob's white pickup truck. They asked Allie and me if we wanted a ride back to the boys' camp. Allie said we didn't. They drove off. Then the two couples, Dalton and Martha with the cooler, Stuart and C.C., headed down the hill to the girls' camp. Allie and I started in a direction perpendicular to theirs. From the barn we went behind Charlie's house and then along the grazing field for the horses to the boys' camp.

"Did you have fun tonight?" I asked.

"Yes. You know I did."

"Good," I said, and nothing more.

We walked a few more steps, and then she turned to me a little. "You're very sweet... Don't worry about me."

"I'm not worried about you. I think about you a lot. You know that, don't you?"

"Yes," she said. "I know."

After that we didn't talk for some time. I was glad I had said it, and I liked her answer more than I didn't. She didn't say she thought about me. I would have liked for her to say it, and I believed it to be so, but I wasn't expecting her to. It was enough for me that I had told her directly, that my cards were on the table.

When we reached the boys' camp, at some point I should have veered off the blacktop walk to the left to go to my cabin. I stayed with her past the boys' main office and then through the playhouse to the infirmary. She didn't question it. Not only that, but when we reached the infirmary, she asked me if I would mind sitting with her on the bench. "I don't want this night to end," she said.

"How can I resist such a nicely painted bench?"

We listened to the crickets chirping for a while. Lightning bugs were all around us, as far as you could see—soft green flashes as pleasing as the end of Gatsby's dock. "Is it a secret," I asked, "where you just came from? I wasn't sure if I was supposed to tell people that."

"No. It's not a secret. C.C. and Martha know. A lot of other people do, too."

"But you don't talk about it, do you?"

"It's not my favorite subject."

"Not tonight, but sometime, will you tell me about it?"

"I'll tell you something now. I believe I saved a life over there, at least one life."

"I don't get what you're saying. I bet you saved hundreds, thousands."

"I mean one person because of me," she said. "The thousands of lives you're talking about, another nurse would have been there to save those. I think I saved at least one person because I was a good nurse. I can't say which patient it was, but I believe a soul is out there because I did something another nurse wouldn't have."

I told her I understood, and that it was a good thing having a soul in the world on her account. We listened to the rhythmic chirping of the crickets a little while longer.

"I know you want to call it a night," she said.

She rose from the bench, and I did the same, so we were standing just a couple of feet apart. Without hesitating, Allie narrowed the distance between us and then lifted her face to press a kiss to my lips. It may have been a quick short kiss, but it was a kiss.

"You need to meet a girl your own age," she said in a soft voice. "But if you find one here, I'll be jealous."

Chapter Three

Other than in the mess hall, I didn't see Allie again for the rest of first period. She didn't come to the Tuesday or Thursday night mixer. I was busy, though. I think I slept out in the woods with my kids four nights that first period. One night was kind of mandatory. A good counselor would do two. Only a rookie would do three, and four was absurd. I don't think I ever did more than two the rest of the summer. They were fun at first, though. We alternated between bringing watermelon or s'mores.

Kind of a neat thing happened at the end of the period. I had no idea Timmy Campbell was decorating a leather belt for Dalton at handicraft. When Timmy gave it to him, Dalton almost started crying. He put it right on. Timmy had stained the belt and punched the edges, and Dalton's name was right in the middle of the back of it.

At the Thursday mixer, C.C. was now in the habit of informing me without asking. "She's not coming," was becoming a mantra. Later that night, when the basement was clearing out, C.C. and I sat together on the shuffleboard table with our backs against the wall. "I don't know what to think about her," C.C. said, not needing to identify Allie by name.

We sat there a little while longer, and then C.C. volunteered, "I probably shouldn't tell you this. A couple of nights ago, I went over to the infirmary, and she had been crying—really hard, I think." C.C. explained that she and Martha often visited Allie at the infirmary. On this night, however, C.C. had come later than usual, so late that Allie didn't think anyone was coming.

"When you guys are talking on a normal night," I asked, "do you get the idea anything's wrong?"

"No. We just talk, and she's one of us."

"Have you ever seen her drink? Liquor, I mean?"

"No."

I told C.C. the story. I didn't think I would ever tell that to anyone, but I told her, all the while feeling horrible about doing it. "When you saw she had been crying, did you ask her?"

"I tried. I didn't get anything out of her. Not a word. Whatever it is, she's not ready. The other night would have been a good time to do it, if she was going to tell me. Maybe she'll tell you someday."

"Me? I don't even see her, except at the mess hall."

"It's not going to be me... She doesn't talk about you. Sorry to burst your bubble. But she has a crush on you, too. Don't give up on her yet, Jake. You should keep trying."

"Dalton and Stuart tell me I'm crazy."

"What do those two idiots know about women?"

* * * * *

Saturday morning at eleven-thirty, all of us were paid in cash at the main office in the boys' camp, minus beer money from the mixers. After we were paid, the girls walked back down to their camp, and the guys just lingered around for a while. No one was allowed to leave until Bernie and Sister Helen, respectively, made an announcement over the loudspeakers at noon. Bernie's was usually like, "All right, guys, you got twenty-four hours. Don't do anything stupid." I never heard Sister Helen's, but I'm sure it was more uplifting.

We were from all around the city, but most of us had about a forty-minute drive home, or less. It was kind of strange, being out of Fort Ross. For me, it had been almost three weeks since I had left the place. Truly, it was nice to be out of there. I got some home-cooking and clean clothes and even touched base with some television, the national news. Except for Charlie and perhaps Father White, I don't think there was a TV in all of Fort Ross.

Allie had attended a wedding shower for her sister over the break, she told me in the mess hall. Thank God I could see her in the mess hall, at least. Allie ate with Bernie, Father White, Sister Jean, and the two assistant directors of the boys' camp, older college guys. Sister Jean managed the accounts of the entire camp from the main office in the boys' camp. The boys' mess hall was much closer for Allie. She was kind of considered 'administration,' too. For whatever group of reasons, I was glad she ate with us. It was my only salvation.

Stuart and I stayed together for the second period, and so did C.C. and Martha. Not only that, but we both had senior cabins, with twenty-five to thirty in each. Senior campers were aged fourteen and fifteen, and there was a lot of socializing between the two, which meant Stuart and I were able to spend time with C.C. and Martha. Allie came to help chaperone the night we had a dance in the playhouse, and we needed her to patrol the nature wings on either side of the basketball court. Martha was shocked, wide-eyed. "These kids are *how old?*"

On the middle Saturday of second period, it had been two weeks since the night of the campfire. I knocked on the infirmary door at about nine o'clock. It was just getting dark. Dylan wafted out. Allie smiled when she saw me and welcomed me in. She asked if I wanted some cold watermelon from her fridge. I did. We sat at her desk, with just me eating, and inelegantly spitting out black seeds.

"I never get to see you," I said. "I've been thinking about poisoning a kid. So far, I haven't gotten so much as a headache out of them."

"You can visit me any time," she answered.

"I've been pretty good, haven't I, about not bothering you?"

"You have."

"Will you go horseback riding with me?"

"Oh, Jake."

"Come on... Dalton, Stuart and I have been riding lots of times. It's fun."

"Aside from everything else, I don't like horses. They're kind of scary."

I didn't think that would be my problem, but I was ready for it. "Most of the horses here are old nags. They know they're putting city kids on them. About ten of them are spirited for the riding staff. The rest are just about dead. We'll saddle the oldest, gentlest nag they can find."

She didn't say anything for a while. "What about the rest of it? If you're thinking about me, you won't meet anyone else."

"I'm just talking about a little horse ride. Have you even been out in the woods? This is really a neat place, Allie. You ought to take advantage of it. You ought to enjoy some of it, more than you and C.C. playing tennis, when you can do that anywhere."

"You're going to be a good lawyer some day."

"Does that mean yes?"

She hesitated. "All right... Just this once."

I picked up Allie at the infirmary at two o'clock. I was clear for most of the afternoon. My kids were scheduled. Allie was ready and waiting for me. I had never seen her in jeans, which I had told her to wear. She looked shorter—of course, I didn't say that. She looked very nice in jeans, especially her backside. Her blonde hair was pulled back, as usual.

"I can't believe you're getting me on a horse," she said with a mixture of excitement and trepidation.

Before leaving the infirmary, Allie had rolled up a red bandanna, doused it with water and tied it around her neck, for it was very hot and humid. "It'll probably be dry by the time we get to the stable," she said. I liked very much the way it looked around her long, graceful neck.

The afternoon sun was beating down as we stepped outside. It was just blistering. We walked through the playhouse and then took the blacktop path past the boys' office and then to the mess hall. Once beyond the mess hall we could see across the baseball field to the stable. Two horses were saddled and waiting for us.

I had asked a friend in the riding department to select the gentlest horse there was for Allie. I also asked him to saddle and bridle it, and mine, too. With Dalton and Stuart, we saddled and bridled our own, but I could never get the dang saddle tight enough. Horses bloat their bellies as a trick. I wanted to make sure Allie's saddle was on there right.

As we crossed the baseball field to the stable, my buddy who had prepped the saddles rode over to tell us which was Allie's horse, and then he trotted off for afternoon program. One was brown, the other a paint. Allie was supposed to take the brown one.

We approached them from behind. My paint was much taller than the brown one. Neither looked any great shakes from behind—boney, hippy. When we got around to the front of them, though, I had to start laughing, because Allie's ride was the most pathetic piece of horseflesh you have ever seen. It had to be at least twenty years old, small, scrawny, ribs showing, big swayback hips. The ears went way more sideways than up. The most disturbing thing was its nose, and above it was bright pink. Its eyes were lined with pink as well. It had thick gray eyelashes.

"He's cute," Allie said.

"Don't ever call me cute," I replied.

"What's his name? Do you know?"

"Elmer," I said with a laugh.

"He's not glue yet." She petted him on his pink nose.

I told her they didn't always name camper horses, although this one should have a name. "I know what I'm going to call him," she said. "Thunder."

We both started laughing.

Allie mounted with ease. I held the reins while she put both hands on the saddle horn. The stirrup was a little high for her, even on a small horse, but she slid her left foot in and popped up into the saddle. "How is it up there?" I asked.

"Good. This is good."

From the stable, we rode side by side at a slow pace behind the boys' Cabins 18–10 to get to the woods. My paint left me considerably higher than Allie in the saddle. It was no prize, either—another camper horse. "Do you think Thunder is going to make it?" I asked.

"He's ready to run a marathon," Allie replied.

"It's a good thing you don't weigh an ounce more... How much do you weigh, anyway?"

"Jake, you don't ask a woman her weight. You know that. You already asked me how old I was."

"What are you worried about? You're *perfect*. I'm asking what perfection weighs."

She turned to me with half a smile. "Don't start saying funny things, okay?"

"Okay."

I let a few seconds pass before I said, "A hundred and ten."

"A hundred and *eight*," she said quickly.

When we entered into the woods, it was like air conditioning, being out of the sun with a pleasant breeze. For a while we were able to ride side by side. Eventually, however, the trail narrowed to where one of us had to lead. We pulled to a stop. "I should probably go first," I said. "But that means I can't keep an eye on you."

"I'm doing fine," she said. "You know where we're going, I hope."

My paint slid in front of her, and we continued at a dead slow walk. No matter where you went in the woods, you came to hills, and we did—first down a steep one, and then back up. "That was fun," Allie said. "This is the way to see the woods."

I turned around. "Is Thunder still breathing?"

"He's a noble steed."

Riding like this wasn't exactly conducive to talking, and we didn't for a while. We just plodded along and took in the sun-dappled scenery, with a nice breeze keeping us company. The birds were singing, and we could hear campers' voices every now and then. There were some huge fat trees in the woods, but mostly the hillsides were graced with much smaller-sized trunks, perhaps four or five inches wide. Of course, the trees grew randomly apart, but at long distances they looked positively uniform, as if planted carefully in a design.

"Are you getting bored?" Allie asked.

"What do you mean?"

"When you go riding with Dalton and Stuart, you run them, don't you?"

"We do." I turned around to see her. "I don't care. I'd rather ride with you than Dalton and Stuart any day."

We continued on at our same steady pace until we reached a wide creek bed. I pulled my paint to a stop and let Allie come along aside of me. "We've been riding about a half hour," I said. "With the ride back, you're going to be saddle-sore if we keep on. You're going to be saddle-sore anyway."

"I suppose there's Thunder to think about, too," she said.

We turned our horses around, but that was all the further we went, still in the wide, rocky creek bed. Water was rushing real fast at one spot. You could hear it. "Hold on a second," I said. I dismounted. "Give me your bandanna. I'll get it wet in the creek."

"You make me feel guilty," she said, starting to untie it. "I have a blue one. I should have brought it for you."

"I wouldn't wear it anyway. They look good on girls."

She handed me her red bandanna, and I took it to where the water was rushing, a few yards away. Giving it back to her, I said, "It was really cold water."

She draped it around her neck and sighed. As I was stepping away from her, she said, "Here. Feel it." I stepped back to her, to where she could press it to my forehead, just long enough to appreciate its coolness, and then she drew it away. As she was wrapping it around her neck again, she said, "Jake, you're going to make some girl awfully happy."

I remained standing where I was, right next to her. "But not you this summer, right?"

"Right." She was tying it now.

"You can't blame me for trying."

"I don't."

What else could I do but get back on my horse? But I was gaining on her, I believed. The idea of us being together was no longer totally outrageous. We were moving toward improbable. I would settle for that, for now.

We had a nice ride back, too, slow, steady. The whole ride we never went beyond a walk, and I could have cared less. The sun was beating down when we got out of the woods, but at least we could ride side by side. "Thunder's still going strong," Allie said.

"We'll be eating him next week," I replied.

I dreaded the sight of the stable, but it came. A spirited horse would start getting frisky at the sight of the stable, but not these two. We plodded to the very end. "Well," she said, with about twenty yards to go, "you got me back safe."

"Who are you talking to—me or Thunder?"

"Both... Thank you, Jake. I probably wouldn't have done it all summer, if not for you."

We dismounted at the same time and experienced it together, the first couple of steps on the ground with your legs finally back together. "Lord," Allie said. "What have you done to me?"

First, we walked ourselves off, and then we took the saddles off and walked the horses dry in the baseball field, which only took a couple of minutes. With Dalton and Stuart, it might be a half hour. Allie sat on the fence while I took them both through the stable and out into the pasture.

When I returned, I said, "Thunder just collapsed."

She laughed. "He'd better not. If I ever go riding again, I'm taking him."

I knew better than to say we should do it again. I knew I was lucky she had accepted my invitation once. I couldn't knock on the infirmary door again for anything like this. "Will you come to the mixers sometime?" I asked.

"We'll see."

"I know what that means."

After dinner that night, Allie came up to me outside the mess hall. "Here," she said, with a blue bandanna in her hand.

I took it from her. "Are you sure?" I asked. "You know I won't wear it."

"I'm sure," she said. "Blue's not my color. It's for you."

* * * * *

At the Thursday night mixer—at which Allie didn't show, of course—C.C. told me her birthday was coming in the middle of next period. At least I could knock on her door for her birthday, but that was more than a week away. After she gave me the bandanna, I didn't talk to her all week. Then a small door opened, from out of the blue.

On Friday night, the last of second period, she caught up with me outside the mess hall. "Guess what?"

she said excitedly. "I'm doing the scenery for the variety show."

Every period had a special event on the last Thursday, which parents attended. One was a rodeo, another was Olympic Day. But the big event of the summer was the variety show, third period. The show took place on the wide apron of the boys' swimming pool, which had a natural amphitheater around it.

"I guess I mentioned to someone that I could draw," she said. "They were more than happy to push it on me."

I was excited for her. I could feel her enthusiasm. Then I had something to be glad about. She told me that she was going to do the painting in the barn, and that the old panels for the scenery were rotting out, so Dalton and I would build her new ones. "He volunteered you."

"I would have volunteered myself," I said. "Do you know what it's going to be yet?"

"I think so. 'Animal Kingdom,' that's the theme of the show."

There was a God in heaven, I thought, walking away from her. Of course, it wasn't any major breakthrough, but it was something—a few more stretches where I could be around her. I couldn't ask for anything more.

Dalton, Allie and I met on Incoming Sunday evening at the barn. How many panels, how high and wide, had to be determined. Allie showed us her sketch. She could draw. She was very talented. The sketch was of Noah's ark, Noah, and all the animals marching in.

"Is it too simple?" she asked.

"No," I said. "I like it."

"That's *awesome*," Dalton said, showing me up.

The old panels were eight feet by eight feet. Dalton said we should probably stick to that. Allie figured five panels would do it. We cleared out two walls in the barn, where they would rest as she painted them. Three panels would go on one wall, two on another. Dalton had only one good moveable light that was truly bright. Allie said it was all she needed, along with a stepladder.

By Monday night, Dalton and I had a panel finished and were completing another. We were waiting for Allie to come—or I was, after her night call. "You owe me one, Jake," Dalton said. "The old panels weren't that bad. Or we probably could have gotten another year out of them."

Dalton and I were working in an open area just inside the sliding doors when Allie arrived. Dalton's radio was blasting hard rock, The Allman Brothers presently. "I can't wait to get started," she said.

I turned to Dalton. "What's she going to do? She only listens to Bob Dylan."

"*Who?*" Dalton exclaimed, well aware of her listening habits.

"I think her ears might fall off."

"Pearls before swine, boys. Pearls before swine... And I can smell the pigs to prove it."

The barn did have an earthy smell, mostly of fresh hay up in the loft. There was plenty of stuff in it, lawnmowers, an old tractor. Dalton had cleared a corner for her. She went straight to it. Her paint cans were there, some gallon-sized, most quarts. Dalton had transported them for her when picking up her garbage. "It's all there," he said.

"I know. I know. I'm just checking again, to see what I have." She opened a quart.

I could tell this was important to her. And I could also see she was doing much better in her general frame of mind. She just seemed happier than the day I met her, more carefree, more at ease with herself. I would have liked to say I had something to do with it, but I knew I didn't. A month of relaxing at this place had done a world of good for her.

Allie was in the barn about five minutes when Dylan's "Like a Rolling Stone" came over the radio. She bounced up from her paint cans and pointed at us and started laughing. "You guys, tell me this isn't a great song," she said with a challenge. Neither of us challenged it. How do you challenge 'Like a Rolling Stone'?

"He got lucky," Dalton said.

Allie sang along for about half of it, just to annoy us, I think. Dalton told her Linda Ronstadt didn't have anything to worry about.

The first panel was already against the wall, where she would paint it. When Dalton and I completed the second panel, we placed it right next to it. Allie didn't do any painting that night, while Dalton and I were working on the third panel. On her stepladder she measured and marked her two panels. A lot of the night she spent in her corner, with the bright light Dalton had given her, mixing colors. White cardboard was stapled to the panels when we finished them. She had a decent-sized piece of it on top of a bale of hay, trying colors out.

When we finished the third panel, Dalton was ready to call it a night, which meant I was, because I was merely assisting. "You guys want a ride?" he asked.

Allie said she was going to continue experimenting for a while, searching for the perfect brown for the ark. "It takes so long to dry. You can't tell what a color is until it dries."

I told Dalton to go on. Then I went down into the basement, where fans kept the pigs cool. I brought a fan with an extension cord up for her. She didn't see what I was doing, hunched over the paint cans with her back to me. I took her cardboard sheet with the drying colors, stood it on the side of the bale of hay, and switched on the fan.

"That'll *work*," she said, turning around. "Thank you, Jake."

"I didn't know you were such an artist."

"I'm not. I love it, though. I took some courses in high school, at a museum on Saturdays."

"There's so much I'd like to know about you," I said.

Allie tried to make light of it. "You know how much I *weigh*. What else do you need to know?"

I was well aware there was no point in pushing it. I was grateful for the time I could spend with her. "I'm going to take off," I said. "You know I don't want to, right?"

"I know." She stood and faced me. "Thanks for the fan, Jake. You always seem to know the right way to help me."

I thought of kissing her. I wanted to kiss her. I looked at her a long second, at that gentle slope of her nose and her enormous green eyes, and then I said the only thing I could. "You're welcome."

I saw her at the barn the next night, too, but not for very long. She had to take care of her night call, and I was on duty for cabin-walk at nine. In the half hour we were there together, I managed to bang my left thumb with a hammer, because I had one eye on her, I know. I dropped the hammer and circled the barn floor with a few choice words—more than a few, actually—because Allie was smiling and Dalton was laughing when I finished.

"Jake," Allie said, "I didn't know you could talk like that."

"*All* the time," Dalton said. "The chickens blush."

While I reminded Dalton that Charlie had no chickens, Allie looked my thumb over. It wasn't that bad, not in need of medical attention. "You'll live," she said, and then added, "I'm *crushed!* You better wash that mouth out with soap."

* * * * *

Once the five panels were done, I was finished at the barn. I never saw Allie put color on any of them. She was at the barn most of the week. The whole camp was alive with the variety show. Dalton, Stevie and Uncle Bob used posthole diggers to erect a structure for the lights. Different acts rehearsed in the playhouse and mess halls. Almost day to night, over the loudspeakers came songs from the performance. I bet they played "I Want a Hippopotamus for Christmas" a hundred times, with "Nashville Cats" and Elvis' "Hound Dog" closely behind.

Allie's presence at the barn worked for me. When C.C. told me about Allie's birthday, she said she was planning a cake. I thought of something else to do for Allie, shortly after I was informed. At the campfire, she had said she loved fires. My idea was to build her a campfire site, in the woods behind the infirmary. Only about ten feet of grass were behind the infirmary before the woods started—not enough room there. About thirty yards into the woods, however, was a perfect flat open area down a little from the infirmary and around a big tree.

When I asked Dalton for his help, I thought maybe I was going to the well once too often, but he was all for it. By the time we finished talking, he had visions of building the Astrodome. It truly wasn't all that much work. We raked the area of leaves and dug a pit. From a creek across the road from camp, we gathered fieldstones to line it. The hardest part was getting three suitable tree trunks down there. Dalton, Stevie, and Uncle Bob did it while Allie was at the mess hall. When they dragged the tree trunks, it made a nice start of a trail.

There were no windows on the back of the infirmary, where Bob Dylan's poster was displayed, so there was no way Allie could see what was going on. For an hour of recreation time I had my nine campers gather firewood. I was almost certain she was at the barn, but we kind of sneaked around to be safe, as much as eight-year-old kids can be quiet for an hour. In the unlikely event she was in the infirmary, she couldn't see us, anyway.

Allie's birthday wasn't a secret. They announced it in the mess hall at lunch, and we all sang to her. I wished her a happy birthday at two of the three meals. I'm certain she wasn't expecting anything else. At about ten o'clock, the five of us huddled outside the screen door of the infirmary while lighting the candles, me, C.C., Stuart, Dalton and Martha. Dalton was holding the cake, of course, a huge sheet cake with white frosting. No matter what, he would have been the one carrying it, but in this case he was the one who had gone out and purchased it. Dalton could leave camp any time. The rest of us needed almost an Act of Congress.

We went in singing. Allie came out of her back room with a pleased smile on her face. "You guys," she said when we finished singing.

"Blow out the candles," Dalton said. "We got a forest fire here. How old are you?"

Allie blew them out. White smoke rose from the white cake.

"Did you make a wish?" Dalton asked.

"Yes, Dalton. I did."

I wondered if I was a part of that wish. Probably I wasn't, but I hoped I was.

Allie was culling paper plates and plastic forks when Dalton said we would eat *al fresco.* "Okay," Allie replied. She was thinking we would sit on the bench. When we stepped outside, we kept walking, and before Allie could muster a question, Dalton told her, "You'll see."

Allie didn't say anything as we started into the woods on a trail that hadn't existed ten hours before. Dalton was first in line, of course. I was second, and Allie was third. He had built an extra-big fire, which was blazing as we approached. The entire site was lit up. He had used a chain saw to flatten the tops of the three tree trunks, so they were inviting to sit upon. The pile of wood looked massive. If she had a fire every night, she still might not need any more. Last but not least, and a surprise to me, were two cheap lawn chairs that filled out the open end.

Allie kept walking after she knew there was a fire, but she stopped at the clearing. As soon as she stopped, she started tearing up. "Happy birthday," Dalton said.

C.C. pulled her to her for a moment and kissed her on the cheek. "Do you like it?"

"Yes," Allie said softly. "Oh, yes." She didn't move, so no one else did, either. She stood there, wiping the tears from her eyes.

"Come on, quit your blubbering," Dalton said. "We got cake to eat." He set the cake on the arms of one of the lawn chairs. It was a massive sheet cake, about ten times too big.

"Where did the lawn chairs come from?" I asked Dalton.

"Father White. They've been sitting on his porch folded up behind a table all summer."

"You'll get in trouble one of these days," C.C. said. "How much money are you worth?"

"I'm a utilitarian, C.C. Waste not, want not. That's what Charlie says."

We sat three to a tree trunk, eating Allie's cake. She and I were on different trunks, but next to each other, with about a two-foot opening where you stepped in. She wanted to know when all this was done. Dalton let her know in no uncertain terms how difficult it had been dragging the tree trunks. He did give Stevie and Uncle Bob a little bit of credit, too. "We were like mules. *Mules!*" As for my contributions, I was left completely out of the equation.

C.C. was looking out for me. "It was Jake's idea, Allie. He's the one who thought of it."

Allie turned to me and said in a soft voice, "Thank you." She didn't say anything more. Instead she put her hand on my shoulder and left it there for a little while, massaging it gently. I thought she might start crying again, but she was able to hold it off. What she managed when she was looking at me was a sad smile.

Dalton had a second piece of cake, and that was as long as the four of them stayed. "Are you ready to roll, Cecilia?" Stuart said. Dalton and Martha caught the same wave out.

All four kissed Allie on her cheek before they left. C.C. gave her a big hug, too. "Happy birthday, Allie," I heard her whisper.

Allie and I were left standing there. "You're going to stay, aren't you?" she asked.

"Do you want me to stay?"

"Yes."

We sat on a tree trunk fairly close together, maybe six inches, and looked into the fire for a long time. I think I was afraid to say anything. She wanted me to stay. I was so far up in the thin air I needed to get used to it. I believed she was trying to as well.

"What am I going to do about you?" she said finally, still looking at the fire.

"You make it sound like a curse," I answered.

"I'm another year older, you know. Couldn't you be at least *twenty?*"

There was another long pause, where we gazed at the cackling fire. I didn't feel the need to say anything now. I was winning this contest, I knew. I could tell.

"Tonight is a low blow," she said, still looking at the fire. "I mean it. *Entirely* below the belt. You don't fight fair... Why do you have to be such a good kid?"

"I don't know about that. I'm not sure I deserve an award for tonight. Yeah, I went to some trouble, but look where it got me, sitting here alone with you in front of this campfire."

"That's not why you did it. You're not that devious. I told you I loved fires... You're smart, but you're not devious. That's one of the things I love about you."

The whole time she was looking in the fire. I turned to her more than once, but she never turned to me, until now, with her big green eyes. "I want you to kiss me," she said. "But just a little. Do you think you can do that?"

"Yes," I answered. "I can do that. It's about all I know."

She seemed to like the answer. She gave me a small smile, and I kissed her. I didn't touch her anywhere else. I bent my head down a little and pressed against her warm, soft lips. She kissed me back, pressing against me just a little harder, just enough to let me know she was there. I'm not sure how long it lasted—five seconds, maybe ten. I know I felt the most pleasing warmth spread all over my body that I never had before. I had kissed some girls, not that many, but it had never felt like this.

"You can put your arms around me," she said softly, "if you want."

I turned more to her and put my arms around her and started gently stroking her back. "Yes," she whispered in my ear. "That's nice."

I could feel her breathing. I could feel her heart beating. For a long time, I held her like that. She gave her weight to me, and I was aware of her breasts pressing against my chest. She started moving her hands across my back, too, very lightly.

We kissed again, this time just a little more intensely, for my arms were around her now. I felt her tongue brush across my lips, but just briefly, and then she stopped kissing me. "You are such a good boy," she said with satisfaction.

"I wish you would stop calling me 'boy' and 'kid.' That's not helping."

"It's what you are. I know I complain about your age, but I don't want you to grow up. Ever."

Chapter Four

On the middle Saturday of third period, Dalton pulled up in his battered blue Ford. My cabin and another were engaged in a game of 'peace' ball on the boys' tennis courts way back where the boys' woods began. The game was truly dodgeball. After many summers of it being called 'war' ball at Fort Ross, it had now transitioned to 'peace' ball.

"Want to do some work for a change?" Dalton asked me. I was sitting in the shade with the counselor whose cabin we were competing with. He didn't care. I got in. Wherever we were going, I hoped, it would be out of earshot of "I Want A Hippopotamus For Christmas."

We kind of did what we wanted, within reason. If you needed to take off for something, there was always someone around to look after your kids. Most of the counselors were very good with the kids, but there were moments where you had to laugh. Peace ball, for example. On super-hot days, veteran counselors were known to pull their cars up to the tennis courts and sit in the air conditioning as the mortal struggle ensued. Disputed calls were settled with a honk of the horn. The winners got five minutes to sit in the car.

When we reached the barn, Dalton placed a hoe in my hand. Charlie had a ten-acre cornfield. Every day except Sunday, Dalton, Stevie and Uncle Bob cultivated three rows, each over a hundred yards. The cornfield was in the front lower part of camp not that far from the barn, but we drove down anyway. With a plastic milk-jug of water, we started into the head-high field.

"Charlie's got cancer," Dalton said, almost right away. "He's going to the hospital tomorrow. I don't think he's ever coming back."

At least now I understood what I was doing here. I took it as a compliment. Dalton had helped me in so many ways. I wished there was some way I could help him now. If there was, I couldn't think of it.

"I knew this was my last summer," Dalton said. "I never figured it would be Charlie's, too."

Dalton wanted to talk, and I listened. Charlie was apparently something of a terror—strict, stern. Dalton started working for him in pre-camp maintenance, as I did, intending to be a counselor, and never stopped. Charlie taught him how to drive a nail and to fix screens, windows, toilets, anything that came along.

"I don't know my father very well," Dalton said. "My mother worships the ground I walk on. I'm an only child. But I don't know my old man. He works a lot. He travels all the time."

"You'll be a first," I said. "The president of a conglomerate who's also a handyman."

"I don't intend to work that much," Dalton said. "This is the hardest work I'll ever do."

I was out there for maybe forty-five minutes with him, and that was about all my soft hands could tolerate. I told Dalton I had to get back to my kids.

* * * * *

After Allie and I kissed on her birthday, I left the infirmary shortly thereafter. Both of us sensed, I think, that enough had happened for one evening, for neither of

us expected what had taken place. The next mixer was
Tuesday night. I didn't ask her if she was coming, and
she didn't tell me she was. I believed she was coming,
and I was about as nervous as I had ever been. As much
as I wanted it to happen, I just couldn't believe it was.
The way I figured it, I was about halfway up Mt. Everest,
flip-flops and all. As much as I wanted to keep my eyes
on the summit, I think I was still looking down at the
drop.

When I arrived at the basement of the boys' shack,
C.C. came straight up to me, as she usually did, to let me
know Allie wasn't coming. Tonight, however, she said,
"You guys kissed, didn't you?"

"Did she tell you that?"

"Yes... You're *good* for her."

"Does Stuart know? I haven't said anything, and
especially not to Dalton. I don't want anything that would
scare her off."

"Martha knows. That's all."

Allie came in behind Martha. Right away my heart
started fluttering. I had a hard time believing she was
here for me, but she was. She was wearing the same
white sleeveless linen blouse she had worn at the initial
mixer. She stood out a little in it. Most of the girls had
long since abandoned their blouses for T-shirts. Allie
looked as fresh and new as opening night, a shiny penny
from heaven.

Dalton and I were standing with Stuart and C.C. when
they joined us. "Look what the cat dragged in," Dalton
said.

Allie placed herself immediately to my side. "Hi," she
said, bashful. "Remember me?" She didn't say hello to
anyone else, just me. Her blonde hair was down, and she

was wearing just a little bit of makeup around her big green eyes. That gentle slope of her nose was as bewitching as ever.

"I'm glad you came," I said.

Dalton and Martha, C.C. and Stuart, they faded away, and we were standing there alone. "I could have worn something else," she said, "but Martha wanted me to wear this again."

"You look amazing."

There was definitely something different about her tonight. I could tell it right away, an uncertainty, a shyness I had never seen before. Allie could be quiet, but always there was a confidence in her silence, in her bearing. Not tonight. She was nervous.

It made me more nervous—I was expecting her to be the one with a firm handle on things. "I'm glad you're here," I said, unable to keep from repeating myself. "You are so beautiful."

"Thank you," she said with a soft voice. "You make me feel that way."

"Would you like to dance?" I asked.

"Yes," she answered softly.

A slow song by Paul Simon was playing, one with a haunting melody that began with the words, "I'd rather be a sparrow than a snail." Allie and I stepped past the thumper table, the number of players diminished by half from the first night, to the back of the basement, where it was most dark. I put my arms around her back, she did the same to me, and we swayed to the music.

Her hair smelled like strawberries. That was about all I would remember from the two-plus minutes I held her. I put my arms around her and smelled her hair, and then the music was over.

"You are such a tiny little thing," I said.

"I like to think I'm two inches short of five foot five... How tall are you?"

I smiled. "That's kind of a personal question, isn't it?"

She let a moment pass and then said, "Five foot seven."

"Six even," I replied, but not as quickly as she had responded about her weight.

After that I think we were both more comfortable. We didn't spend time in a corner talking together, or anything like that. We kind of stayed together, but with different people around.

Dalton was a Nixon supporter, and we listened to him defend the President to all comers. "McGovern?" he said. "You *got* to be kidding me." Dalton may have been the only one for Nixon, but he held his ground. "We only have one President at a time. You got to support him." He called everybody else "peaceniks" and said the peace symbol was "the footprint of the great American chicken." Then somebody asked Dalton about his plans for law school, if the draft was still in effect.

I watched Allie carefully when it came to this subject. It didn't seem to bother her. She was interested in what was being said, but it didn't seem to disturb her or make her uncomfortable. I was glad about that.

"Can I walk you home?" I asked at that end of the night. I didn't want to presume anything, and I think she appreciated it.

"Yes," Allie said. "I would like that."

As we left the basement, she went first up the concrete ramp, and I followed. Three or four people were sitting outside on the concrete wall, but none of them happened to be Dalton Talbott, which was all I cared about, because God only knows what he would have said. As soon as we stepped into the darkness, I reached for Allie's hand, and she let me take it.

The distance from the boys' shack to the infirmary was just a couple of hundred yards. I could have walked through the Sahara with her holding her hand. "Let's sit for a while," she said, when we reached our destination. We sat on the white bench still holding hands. The crickets were chirping in cadence, and the lightning bugs were all around, just like during the first night she lightly kissed me after the campfire in the woods.

"I think I could hold your hand forever," I said. "You're never getting it back."

"I like holding yours, too," she replied. "I like it a lot." In spite of what she said, there was a shyness in her tone, as at the beginning of the evening and still some throughout it, a vulnerability she normally didn't present. "Martha and C.C. are expecting a full report," she said, "so we'd better behave ourselves. Okay?"

"Okay," I answered.

Then we started kissing. I moved slowly toward her as she moved toward me, and we pressed our lips softly together. I put my arms around her, and she did the same to me, but not very tightly, my chest barely touching hers. We kissed that way for a long while, and then gradually it deepened, as did my hold on her. I felt her tongue flit across my lips, and then my tongue was touching hers. A familiar warmth spread throughout me.

We kissed with our tongues exploring for a very long time, and then I put my hand on her breast. She let out a small murmur, partly in surprise but mostly in appreciation, letting me know it was okay. I touched her there gently at first, as if I were afraid she was going to change her mind. I just couldn't believe this was happening.

She murmured again when I took it fully. Almost right away her nipple hardened. I pulled a little away from her. "Does that feel good?" I asked.

"Oh, yes," she whispered softly.

"I like *that*," I said.

She gave a soft laugh. "You are *such...* a boy," she said. "I know you don't like hearing me say it, but you are such a boy."

My fingers were still playing with her nipple. "Right now, I don't care what you call me. Call me Richard Nixon."

She smiled at me, and then she stilled my hand. "That's enough for tonight, Jacob."

* * * * *

On Wednesday, the day before the performance, over the loudspeakers came a heavy dose of Michael Jackson's "Rockin' Robin" and Henry Mancini's *Pink Panther* theme. Allie had long since finished her painting in the barn, and I was dying to see her work. I wanted her to take me over there, but she wouldn't have it. She said it would be bad luck. I wasn't sure what luck had to do with it.

Of course, I could think of nothing but Allie. A power line cut through one part of the back woods, about a forty-yard clearing of ankle-high grass and very colorful flowers, yellow and purple. It wasn't my intention to pick flowers when I set out on this hike with my campers during recreation time, but it was as soon as I saw them. I don't know what kind of flowers they were. They were most likely weeds, but they had very pretty yellow and purple petals, small petals.

My campers were the same eight-year-old midgets who had gathered her firewood. We were all standing together when I selected the cutest of the lot, the one with the most personality, too, and told him to knock on the screen door of the infirmary. When Allie answered, he raised his gift to her and said, "We picked flowers for the pretty nurse."

Allie stepped out with a huge smile. Each kid had a big bouquet. For each one presented, she bent down and asked the camper's name, and then said, "Thank you," with the name. I gave her my bouquet last. It was way too big, but I didn't really care. With all of those oversized bouquets, she could barely contain them all against her chest. "And what did you say your name was again?" she asked me playfully.

I smiled. "Jacob."

"Thank you, Jacob."

I heard the kids talking to each other about my name change, but I only had eyes for Allie. She gave me a big smile, and then she said, "You're not playing fair again."

* * * * *

You could feel the excitement of show day, even at the morning mess hall. Sometimes breakfast was slumbered through, but not today. Bernie got the kids going early and often. I wish I could accurately relate the amount of power and energy two hundred singing campers could create in that mess hall. I can still hear them singing, "Blood on the saddle, blood on the ground, great big puddles of blood all around, pity the cowboy, bloody and red, the old cowpony done *stomped* on his head!" And with the word "stomped," the wood floor shook like an earthquake, four hundred sneakers crashing down on one word.

Allie was brimming with positivity when I talked to her after breakfast. She said maintenance was hanging the lights first, and then they were bringing over the panels in the cattle truck. The scenery should be up by lunch, she hoped. "I can't wait to see it," I said.

"Me too," she replied. "I can't wait to see it up and all together."

I spent the morning sitting on the front corral near the main gate, filling in for a riding guy involved in the show. By the time I returned to the boys' camp, the scenery was up. I walked from the stable to beyond the boys' mess hall, and I could see the pool down below. All of the panels were up. Dalton was standing to one side of the scenery. Both the blue truck and the white were still parked down there. I figured Stevie and Uncle Bob were behind, bracing the scenery.

The hill around the pool formed a natural amphitheater. I stood right in the center of it to take in Allie's work. It was wonderful, whimsical. Noah was to the far left, with animals at his feet and birds floating around his head. A big brown ark took up the left center, and the right half had animals marching aboard, beginning with giraffes, and then elephants. As the animals got smaller, a lush jungle background grew over them. The grass on which the animals walked was a Kelly green, and the sky was Carolina blue, dotted with puffy white clouds.

As I was looking at it, "Nashville Cats" was playing over the loudspeakers, and Allie came out from behind the scenery. I stayed where I was, and she came up the hill toward me. "Do you like it?" she asked, with some uncertainty.

I let her come all the way to me. "I love it, Allie. I wish the world could be the way you've drawn it here."

"Thank you, Jake."

We stood and looked at it together. I told her how talented she was. She didn't want to hear that. But she did want to know if I truly liked it, and I did my best to convince her I did. "When I was painting it," she said, "I was thinking about you. I wanted you to like it most of all."

* * * * *

The performance began at eight o'clock. Most of the parents arrived between seven and seven-thirty. It was a nice way to start out the evening, seeing supposedly tough little boys running to their mothers after this considerable absence. The campers sat with their parents, of course. I sat on the grass beside Allie, center stage, with my campers, too, the ones whose parents didn't attend. C.C. was on the other side of Allie with her campers.

The show started with a bang: "Rockin Robin." The senior boys and girls danced their hearts out, all dressed alike in blue jeans and plain white T-shirts. It was fun watching them, the upbeat song and the energy of the dancing.

The *Pink Panther* theme was the next number. A band of twelve-year-old boys wearing black Zorro masks outsmarted Inspector Clouseau, who was attired in a long trench raincoat. At the beginning of the music, Clouseau was writing at his desk in a fully furnished office. Then he noticed a chair missing and got up to investigate. Of course, he could never find the bandits moving on and off stage. By the end, everything was gone. The last thing they stole was his desk.

I looked to Allie as we were clapping. She was about as happy as I had ever seen her. Or maybe some of it was me, wishing it on her. I had more than enough happiness to spare. I was sitting next to the most beautiful woman in the world, and every second we spent together, we were getting closer.

Robert John's "The Lion Sleeps Tonight" was followed by Elton John's "Crocodile Rock." The sun was almost all the way down, and the lights illuminated the scenery in the darkness as never before. "Look at it, Allie," I said to her. "You should be so proud."

"Nashville Cats" and "I Want A Hippopotomus For Christmas" went back to back, as they had done all week over the loudspeakers. Probably the cutest act of the night was "Alley Cat," with midget boys and girls dancing together, kinda, sorta in unison. They made a total mess of it, and couldn't have been more endearing in the process. A lot of cats were in the show. "Cat's in the Cradle" was done as a guitar solo by a boy counselor with a deep, powerful voice. By that time it was completely dark. I took Allie's hand for the first time all night, and she she turned to me. She didn't say anything. She just smiled.

The finale was "Hound Dog." About thirty kids rushed onto the stage in Elvis wigs and cardboard electric guitars. There wasn't a lot of choreography in this one; they just kind of jumped and danced around and generally had a good time. At the end of it, anyone who wanted to go onstage and dance could. And they did. Dalton was out there.

Before thanking the parents for their attendance, the master of ceremony recognized Dalton, Stevie and Uncle Bob for their contributions to the sound, lighting and scenery. They came on stage with a quick wave. Allie was recognized, too. She did the same thing. I gave her a standing ovation, through I'm sure she wasn't aware of it.

I didn't talk to Allie after the show. I knew I'd be seeing her at the Thursday night mixer within an hour's time. I rounded up my kids with the goal of getting them in their bunks. They were wound, so I hung around for a while. I knew the mixer wasn't starting on time anyway.

When I arrived in the basement of the boys' shack, C.C. told me Allie wasn't coming. After the show, a camper had come to the infirmary and needed to stay overnight. "That kid better be on death's *door*," I said.

C.C. laughed. "Jake Sullivan, I'm ashamed of you. You've still got fourth and fifth period."

* * * * *

Over the break, Allie had another function with her sister's wedding. Dalton visited Charlie in the hospital. As for me, all I cared about was getting clean clothes and getting back again; Allie would be waiting for me. Even at home I didn't go two consecutive seconds without thinking about her. I honestly didn't know what would happen next, and I couldn't wait to find out.

On Incoming Sunday I was assigned to the playhouse taking temperatures for the first time since opening day. I was ready for Allie in her white uniform and stockings— or I thought I was. Again, she floated into the playhouse in a halo of white. She asked me what I did over the break, and I heard about hers, but it was a brief conversation. When I was talking to her, she was Allie. Watching her leave, however, she floated out of the playhouse in her white halo.

Later in the afternoon, when the playhouse was mostly cleared out, she floated in again. "Why don't you come see me later on?" she said. "I shouldn't have any kids the first night."

"You got it."

"Come about eleven, okay?" she said.

"Okay."

"I'm not telling C.C. and Martha you're coming."

She stayed with me only long enough to gauge my reaction. I'm not sure what I showed—surprise, I suspect, if anything. I was surprised by what she was implying, and also by her sure-footedness. I got the idea she was as disappointed missing Thursday night as I was, and it had created a resolve.

* * * * *

It was a long wait until eleven o'clock. I had butterflies in my belly the size of bats. The last hour I spent sitting on the concrete base of the flagpole with the guys on cabin-walk, just shooting the breeze for a while. It was a black night with no stars. The first night of a session was notorious for a lot of clowning around, and this night didn't disappoint. Probably it was ten-thirty before all cabins were quiet.

At eleven o'clock on the nose, I lifted myself from the concrete base of the flagpole. I walked through the playhouse, and then I could see the infirmary. It was almost completely dark—the business side of it, entirely. A light shone in Allie's back room, an area that took up about a tenth of the structure.

When I knocked on the screen door, she called for me to come in. Enough light was emanating from her room that I could see my way. Bob Dylan's "Subterranean Homesick Blues" was playing softly. Even before I saw her, I could smell the scent of a woman's room. Whatever she had that had been sitting in there all summer, it smelled awfully nice.

When I entered, she was seated at the far end of the bed below the Dylan poster, her legs crossed beneath her. She was barefoot and had on a shiny sleeveless purple blouse and khaki shorts. Her hair was down. Just one small lamp on her night table was on. In a holder was an unlit candle.

"Hi," she said softly. She patted the mattress lightly. "Sit with me. Let's talk for a little while, okay?"

I sat on her bed with my sneakers on the floor. She let a moment or two pass, and then she said, "Well, you've got me where you want me."

"It seems that way," I answered, somewhat in amazement. Going in, I knew it was going to be an important night, but I didn't expect to be where I was five seconds after entering.

"Every now and then, a dog catches the car," Allie said. "Are you sure you're ready? We don't have to do anything if you don't want."

"Is that a trick question? I'm as ready as I'll ever be, I guess. There's no one I would rather... start with. I know that."

Allie looked at me a long second, just kind of taking me in. "All right," she said. "I've done all a card-carrying cradle-robber is obligated to do."

I was aware of my heart beating in my chest. I could feel it pounding. Allie was mine. I knew this was truly going to happen. It was a good thing I was sitting down because I'm not sure my legs could have borne my weight.

"Are you okay with Bob Dylan?" she asked. "Or are your ears going to fall off?"

"I'll risk it," I said with a smile. "You're a nurse. You can fix it."

Allie asked me to light the candle. Once I did, she switched off the small lamp. There wasn't that much difference in the light of the room, but it flickered around with the candle. "We're not finished talking yet," she said. "Take off your sneakers and get comfortable."

I did as she said. When I looked back up to her, for maybe thirty seconds she studied me without speaking, during which neither of us moved a muscle. "Tomorrow I'm going to tell you something," she said, "but I'm afraid I'm going to do it tonight. And I don't want to tell you tonight. Okay?"

Whatever it was, I knew it was serious. I didn't know what to say to it, other than, "Okay."

There was another long interval. Part of it she looked down, and then she raised her green eyes to me, "Your first time should be special."

I wanted to lighten the mood. "You know, I never officially said I'm a virgin."

"You just did about two seconds ago."

"I never said the *word*."

She smiled. "So tell me all about your conquests, you goof."

"Have we talked enough?" I asked.

She took a moment to answer. "I suppose we have."

She uncrossed her legs beneath her and placed her bare feet on the floor next to mine. Then she undid the top button of her blouse and asked if I wanted to do the rest. My hands were shaking some, and the first button took longer than it should have. I asked about the shiny purple fabric that felt so nice, and she said it was silk. With the last button her blouse fell open, and she turned her back to me so I could undo the clasp of her bra.

I lifted the back of her blouse. "I put one on for you, because guys like taking them off," she said, as I worked the clasp clumsily. "Notice I said '*guys.*'"

"It is duly noted and appreciated on both counts."

As she turned back to me, she slipped her bra off and discarded it to the floor.

"Hey, I thought that was my job," I said.

"Do you really want to quibble?" She stood. "Or do you want to take off my shorts?"

I drew her khaki shorts slowly down to her bare feet, where she stepped out of them. She was now standing in front of me in skimpy white panties and an open blouse with no bra on. Then, somehow, things got better. She drew my T-shirt over my head and then put her hand to my chest even before she sat down next to me. Very lightly I felt the tips of her fingers move over my chest and even up to my neck.

"Are you ready, Jacob?" she asked softly.

"I love you," I said simply.

"I love you, too," she whispered. "More than you'll ever know."

We started kissing in the candlelight. Allie's skin had the most wondrous glow as we eased ourselves to horizontal on her bed. We didn't hurry. We even talked some at the beginning. I told her I wanted to undress her from her nurse's uniform, and she laughed.

Before long, the talking was over. Allie was my guide in this new mystic world, of which we were the sole inhabitants. She took me to a place that couldn't even compare to what I had imagined. Gradually we built to it, until we reached a fever pitch. Then I was inside of her, without even realizing it had happened, and we were one. The electricity that had passed between us on the night of the campfire was nothing compared to this. How do you compare a single shock with a connection, a feeling that would echo for a lifetime?

When it was over, we held each other side-by-side for a long while without talking. I had nothing to say and a desperate need to hold her. I don't know how long it was before I opened my eyes and saw the candle flickering. I backed a little away from her face so I could see her. "Did I do okay?"

"Yes," she answered softly. "You were wonderful."

"Good," I said. "It seemed to me it was going pretty well."

"You goof," she replied, and then she drew herself back into me.

What happened next, I had no idea was coming. She started crying, whimpering softly at first, and then it was a full-fledged cry that escalated. I just held her as close as physically possible, and I could feel the depth of it. I could feel it was coming from the very center of her. Whatever it was she had to tell me, I now dreaded hearing it.

It was at least five minutes, maybe twice that, before she started to settle. And then finally she stopped. I was so grateful for it, when her body became as still and quiet as the surface of a pond. She had shed enough tears to fill one.

"Thank you for holding me," she whispered finally in my ear.

"You're welcome," was all I said in reply.

We held each other for a long time without talking, or even seeing each other's faces. I didn't ask, and she didn't volunteer. She pulled away enough so I could see her. "You should be getting back to your cabin now," she said.

"Bernie doesn't know it," I replied, "but the first thing we tell our kids is to go next door if your counselor isn't around. There are two counselors sleeping within five feet of my cabin. I'm not going anywhere."

* * * * *

I slept maybe two hours that night with Allie at the infirmary and woke up with the energy of a bear out of hibernation, and an appetite to match. In the mess hall I think I had six of those little boxes of cereal. In spite of my hunger, I kept an eye on Allie, too. I just couldn't believe it, what we had done together, that she was mine. All summer, the time in the mess hall was when we were closest. From now on, it would be when we were farthest apart.

A heat wave rolled in that afternoon, one for the ages. It was an unusually hot summer in general, and this was its mightiest blow. By one o'clock it was over a hundred degrees. It was so steamy and sticky you could barely move in it, the kind of summer humidity only a Midwestern river valley knows.

After dinner I told Allie I would come by at nine, when cabin-walk started. I wasn't looking forward to it. Instead of butterflies in my belly, I felt a hive of bees. Allie was waiting for me when I stepped inside. She didn't kiss me. She said she wanted to talk in front of the campfire. "It's not hot enough," she said. "Let's build a fire."

Some light was still left as I assembled the twigs and small branches. Allie sat in one of the lawn chairs, watching me. She wasn't saying anything, so I started talking about Dave, who was head of the nature department. Dave wouldn't give you more than one match to start a fire, to ensure that you built it correctly from the beginning.

I was pretty sure it was a one-match fire when I lit it, so I took the lawn chair opposite Allie. We were facing each other some, and the fire, too. "I always like the beginning of a fire," she said, to my everlasting relief. "That's the best part, watching it start."

I agreed, but I didn't have anything to add to it.

For a while she looked at the fire struggling for life, and then she turned to face me. "Something bad happened to me over there," she began simply, and it was a long time before she continued. "I wish I didn't have to tell you about it."

"I want to know," I said. "But you don't have to tell me."

"It was my first week there," she said. "I was green as grass. They use that term in the military a lot. And, boy, was I ever green... Colonel Richard Parker, that was his name. He's probably a general by now."

"Jesus," I said. I had had the day to think about it, and now I knew for sure. I didn't know the details of what had happened, but I knew how it turned out.

"We went to the Officer's Club for dinner. I wasn't aware of it, but he was a big shot. 'This guy is a full-bird colonel,' that's what they kept saying to me. 'A full-bird colonel, you think you're going to ruin his career? Think again. You wanted him to treat you that way.' "

I just listened. I was grateful she was willing to tell me. As hard as it was to hear, the more she talked, the closer I felt to her.

"It was all so practiced," she began again. "We had to go to his quarters because he needed to check on an important cable. God, was I naïve. I bet he did the same thing fifty times before and fifty times since... First, he tried doing it the nice way, and when that didn't work he just grabbed me and threw me down on his living room floor."

"You don't have to go on," I said, but I don't think she even heard me.

"He beat me up and gave me a black eye."

After that she stopped for a while. I wanted to get out of my chair and put my arms around her, but something told me not to. She wasn't finished. Bad as it was, she still had more to say.

"I didn't do enough to stop him, not that night, I mean after it was over. I was shell-shocked, I know, and embarrassed about being so stupid. It haunts me. At night I wonder how many other women he's raped since me."

"It sounds like you tried your best."

"I didn't. After I reported it, I got transferred to another hospital far away. Nothing happened. It just died, and I let it die."

"You shouldn't punish yourself over that asshole. There are assholes all over the place, and other people aren't responsible for what *they* do. You did the best you could, Allie. Nobody is Superman."

"Thank you for listening to me."

Now, I sensed, the time was right to hold her. I took her by the hands first, and then I stood, bringing her up with me. When I put my arms around her, I thought she would start to cry, but she didn't. Maybe it helped her to talk about it. Maybe she was feeling relief that this was over. Or maybe she was just cried out from last night. If anyone was close to tears, it was me.

When we sat down again, it was on a tree trunk. We held hands and looked at the fire. "Last night," she said, "I knew I could trust you. I was as nervous as you were, probably more."

"You didn't act it."

"I figured one of us had to be the adult. I was so sure about you. You gave me the confidence. Call me a cradle-robber. I don't care. I liked you from the first moment I met you, and last night was one of the most special nights of my life."

"Not bad for a kid, huh?"

"Oh, brother," she said. "I've created a monster. We've got the rest of the summer, but not tonight, okay?"

"Okay."

We sat together holding hands until the fire burned down. At the screen door she kissed me on my cheek, and that was all. "Will you do something for me?" she said.

"What?"

"Tell C.C. for me. We'll talk about it when she knows, but I don't want to tell it again."

When I left her, I was certain she was going inside to cry.

* * * * *

I figured I should tell C.C. right away, so Allie wouldn't be wondering. I headed down to the girls' camp the following afternoon, when my kids were at swimming. I learned that C.C. was at the girls' shack, so I headed over there. The girls' shack was in no way convenient to the girls' camp. For whatever reason, it was built almost on top of Father White's house, on the main road coming up. Father White's house was at the right turn to the camps. The girls' shack sat a little before and behind it, and a little farther away from that main road.

Guys were allowed on the large, screened-in porch of the girls' shack, which was actually kind of nice—wicker sofas and chairs with cushions. I didn't want to go in. The porch and its vicinity were always a hub of activity. I thought it might be awkward, telling C.C. that I wanted to talk to her alone. Fortunately, another girl counselor was approaching just as I was. I had her summon C.C. I waited for her about twenty feet from the building.

"You got some time now?" I asked.

"Sure, what's up?"

I hesitated for a moment on purpose. "She told me last night."

"Let's go sit on the well," C.C. said.

Right by the main road, and under a huge old oak, sat an abandoned well of stone and mortar, about three feet high, with a wooden platform on top of it for sitting. Fortunately, in this high heat, the old oak was providing a large area of shade over it, and there was a hint of a breeze. On the face of it, it looked like a very public place. In another way, it was as private as anywhere at Fort Ross. The camps were above us, and no one ever left the place.

I began by saying Allie asked me to relate it. Then I told C.C. everything I knew, without pulling punches, often using Allie's exact words, because they were seared in my brain. C.C. didn't interrupt. When I was finished, her eyes were filled with tears. I just sat there with her quietly. Father White came out of his one-story house and started washing his car.

"You're good for her," C.C. said finally. "You're so good for her."

"I don't think she wants Martha to know," I said. "You can ask her."

We stayed there a little while longer without talking. Perhaps it was the movement that attracted our eyes, because we were both watching Father White tend to his car. "No matter how hot it is, he washes that thing about three times a week," C.C. said, as we were getting down from the platform. "He ought to try himself."

* * * * *

At the Thursday night mixer, C.C., Martha and Allie came as a trio, and Stuart, Dalton and I were waiting for them. Allie had on a red T-shirt, bearing the black letters of the University of Cincinnati, where she had gone to nursing school.

There was a twist to this mixer. It was 'Little Kings night,' a twice-annual event that often led to especially raucous behavior. Normally, 3.2 beer was served at the mixers, in twelve-ounce cans. Little Kings were small green bottles—you could down one in three modest gulps—and considerably more potent.

The other thing that was different was the vicious heat, now in its fourth day. Even the concrete floor of the basement was dry, all the way dry, no dampness at all. And it was actually warm in there with the bodies. A lot of people were sitting outside on the concrete wall that lined the ramp going down, or just standing outside in groups, half in the darkness, with their Little Kings and the music blasting from inside.

Of course, I spent a lot of the evening with Allie, but not nearly all. She knew these people now, too, especially the girls. I didn't care, because she was going home with me at the end of it. Dalton was talking politics again, which was always entertaining. "McGovern can't even pick a vice president," he said. "You gotta be kidding me with this guy."

Near the end of the allotted time, the mixer was still going strong, due to the Little Kings. When Allie asked me if I was ready to leave, I was. We were sitting inside on the picnic table. As we started out of the basement, she took my hand. We walked up the ramp past everyone sitting and standing outside, into the darkness. "I don't care who knows," she said to me, when we reached it. "You're the best guy in this whole camp, and you're mine."

I thought my head might explode from happiness. A single human brain is capable of handling only so much, and she was nearing the limit.

Just the small walk from the boys' shack through the playhouse to the infirmary was enough to heat us up. I don't think either of us thought about going straight inside. We sat on the bench outside, looking down at the boys' pool.

"I never thought I'd be jealous of Charlie's pigs," Allie said, "but I am. I'd love one of those fans for inside."

"Maybe Dalton can get one for you from Father White," I replied. "I'm sure Father White has one lying around, one that hasn't been used *all* summer."

We listened to the crickets chirping and watched the lightning bugs. "This really stinks, you know it?" I said. "We waited so long to get here, and now it's too dang hot to even go inside. Notice I said, '*Dang.*'"

"I guess we'll just have to rough it," she said, with a laugh. "Boy, has this gone downhill fast."

We sat there a little while longer, with neither making a suggestion that we go inside. "There is a perfect solution," I said. "And we're looking at it." I turned to her. "Do you want to?"

"Do I want to what?"

"Let's go swimming. We could slip into the pool real quiet, and not cause a ripple. Once we're in, no one will even know we're in there."

"Yeah... Right."

"Why not?"

"For one thing, like you're not going to take my suit from me. Do you think I'm a moron?"

"I was thinking you could keep your suit *dry*. We'll put it by the side of the pool."

"You've got it all figured out, haven't you? You're just missing one big part."

"Come on. That's what Dalton always says, and it works. Come on, it'll be fun. That water is cool, Allie, so *very* cool. Can't you just feel it, how refreshing it would be, how exhilarating it would feel to slip into a million gallons of *relief* from this madness?"

"Oh, brother," she said in reply. "All right, I'll put my suit on. It seems I'm always putting things on, for you to take off."

Allie came out of the infirmary in a one-piece suit and sandals and carrying a couple of towels. "I can't believe you're getting me to do this," she said.

"I should be a lawyer," I said.

"No. You should be a writer."

We decided the girls' pool was better isolated. The two pools were close to each other, perhaps for the plumbing, and sat like diagonal squares on a chessboard. Whereas you looked down on the boys' pool, most of the girls' pool sat up from the ground some. Just one end was actually level with the ground. A steep bank of grass held up mostly three sides of it.

It was about a hundred-yard walk to the girls' pool. I held her hand and thanked her for going along. She said I had taken care of her with the horses, so she was giving me another chance. We went around to where the pool was level to the ground. Beside it were some bushes and a small set of bleachers. We stood there for maybe thirty seconds, making sure no one was around. The water was flat as a board and had a strong chlorine smell. We did hear the sound of laughter twice, but it was from far away, up in the boys' camp.

"Are we really going to do this?" she asked, with excitement in her voice.

I answered by flipping my T-shirt over my head. I bent down to take off my sneakers. By the time I came back up, Allie had drawn her suit down to her waist and was going farther. "*Again*," I said. "That's supposed to be my job!"

"Shhhh. Shhhh." She started laughing and tried to keep her voice low but didn't really succeed. "All right. All right. I'm nervous about this. I'll pull it back up."

She did, and then I drew it down to where it had been and kissed her. "Are you happy now?" she asked.

"Yes."

We put her suit and my gym shorts by the side of the pool, in case we needed them, and then we slipped into the water at about the four-foot level. Right away we both went under, and it was like turning on a switch, from hot to cold. It was heavenly. Forget about fans and air conditioning. There was nothing in the world that could feel better than this.

"Ohhh," Allie said, as she came up.

"You're welcome," I replied.

She splashed at me and swam away a little, but not too far. She wasn't hard to catch now. It was a whole new sensation with her in the water. She seemed smaller and sexier, because she didn't weigh a pound as I was holding her and kissing her. They were deep, passionate kisses. I started pressing her against the side of the pool.

It was then we heard the sound of horse-hooves. Allie heard them, to be more accurate. I might not have heard an air-raid siren. At first the sound was faint—I don't know *how* she had heard them—but it grew stronger, the unmistakable cadence of a horse trotting toward us.

"Oh, God," Allie said.

"What are you worried about?" I asked. "The horse isn't going swimming. If it's Thunder, that's okay. He's earned a vacation."

We never saw it. With the elevated pool, it passed below us between the pools. We started kissing again, and then we heard what sounded like the Seventh Calvary approaching. I don't know how many horses there were. It had to be four or five, and they were moving at a slow gallop. In the quiet of the night, they were thundering. At least one guy and one girl were laughing as they passed below us.

"Those little green bottles," I said.

"Somebody else is going to be jumping in this pool any minute," Allie replied.

"It's a big pool."

She took me and put me inside of her.

* * * * *

The rest of fourth period, I was with her every moment I could, because she seemed to want me near her. If someone needed to find me, they knew where to look. Allie taught me how to play backgammon. Mostly we played at her desk, and once at her campfire. I got her back up on Thunder. We had another nice slow ride, this time in the girls' woods, which was about twice as hilly as the boys'. We ate cold watermelon from her refrigerator and listened endlessly to Bob Dylan. "I really do like him," I admitted, during that week. "He's an acquired taste."

The special event for fourth period was the Indian Pageant in the front field, otherwise known as 'The Bonfire.' Horses galloped around, and campers performed snake dances in Indian dress. But the big event was the fire. Constructed by the boys' nature department as you would a log cabin, the pyre was maybe fifteen feet high. It was most definitely a one-match, or one-torch, fire, aided by gasoline. At times sparks rose from it at least fifty feet. Allie and I held hands in the darkness and watched it burn.

Three nights in a row that week, Allie had different campers stay over. "It's like the plague," I said. "Two thirds of Europe is now gone."

On Friday, the last of fourth period, I saw an envelope on her desk that was from a hospital in California. When I asked about it, she said she had accepted a job there. "They wanted me to come right away," she said. "But I told them I couldn't, until the Sunday after camp."

I asked her how long she had known. She said about a week. She told me about her new job, and it was obvious she was excited about it. The hospital specialized in patients with severe burns, with which she now had experience. I was only half listening to what she said after that.

"California is so far away," I said. "Have you made plane reservations?"

She nodded.

I didn't want to ask anything more. "Jake, you're getting letters from Ohio State, aren't you? I know. I don't want to think about it, either."

Chapter Five

Driving back to camp on Sunday morning for fifth period, I had clean clothes and a bad feeling. It was impossible not to think about two weeks before. That day, I sensed I was on the verge of catching Allie, and we still had a month of the summer to go. Of course, I wanted desperately to get back to see her. We still had two weeks left. But there seemed to be a black cloud hanging over me, almost an irrational fear I couldn't shake.

The first night of fifth period I was almost guaranteed to have Allie to myself, and that turned out to be the case. We built a fire. Allie had a blue sleeping bag that we spread out like a blanket and sat upon. "There's something I've been meaning to ask you," I said, finally working up the courage.

"What?"

"Do you need a date for your sister's wedding?" It was now six days away. Allie's sister was getting married on the middle Saturday of fifth period. "If I ask now, I can probably get off."

It surprised her. Her green eyes narrowed perceptibly.

"You never even thought about it?" I said.

"No," she answered. "Honestly, no."

"I brought my best and only suit," I said. "I guess I'm not going to be needing it."

"Oh, Jake. I just don't think it would be a good idea. I'm in the wedding. You won't know anyone. You'll be standing around by yourself half the night."

"And you won't have to explain me, either. That's part of it. Isn't it?"

"Yes. It is... What we have is here and only here. It can't leave this place. It can't even travel downtown to a wedding."

There was nothing I could say to it, because it was true. Down deep I knew it, and I knew it more now. I didn't care about not going to the wedding, because Allie was right about that as well. It most probably wouldn't have been a fun night for me. I wanted to be asked much more than I wanted to go.

For a while we watched the fire. She turned to me. "I'm sorry, Jake."

"At least you didn't sugar-coat it."

"This is serious business, Jake, what you and I are playing with. The deeper you fall, the harder it is to get out... I worry about you. I've had my heart broken. That's what it's going to feel like. You're going to break my heart, and I'm going to break yours."

Again, we looked at the fire. Again, nothing came to me to refute a word of what she was saying. "Don't stay mad at me for too long," she said.

"Can I at least see you in your wedding dress? I mean the one you're wearing."

"Yes," she said. "I'll bring it back with me."

I pouted a little while longer. "Okay. I'm not mad anymore."

"We've still got two weeks, Jake. Let's make the very best of it... I know how to kick it off. Why don't we go inside, and I'll put on my nurse's uniform?"

"That's not a bad start," I answered. "Do I get the white stockings, too?"

"Of course."

"Somehow that uniform is going to come off without me having a *thing* to do with it."

She laughed. "Poor baby."

* * * * *

The first week of fifth period flew by. Allie had only one camper stay overnight all week. I didn't spend the night with her, though. She thought I should be in my cabin, so I acceded. We didn't talk any more about the end. Not a word of it.

There was a special event that week, the annual 'Old-Timers' game, where former counselors and staff came to play softball against the present staff. (All guys. This was kind of before co-ed softball.) It was a highly competitive event, and Allie was looking forward to it, being the baseball fan she was. Even the girls' camp came up to watch the game, which was a joke, because the boy campers didn't care who won, and the girls were apoplectic.

"You're going to hit a home run for me, aren't you?" Allie asked.

"Look at me," I replied, with my palms out. "Do you see any meat on these bones?"

"Still... If you *loved* me..."

As it turned out, I didn't even get an 'at bat,' and I was okay with it, more than okay, considering Allie's expectations. I didn't know any of the guys we were playing against, and the older counselors did, so they played. The 'Old-Timers' ended up winning it, in a close one. Most of the 'Old-Timers' looked just a little older than us, but several were in their thirties and forties, and a score or more of that age were watching. After the game, they all went out drinking.

Allie left camp on Friday at noon for her sister's wedding. The rehearsal dinner was Friday night, and the wedding was scheduled for late afternoon. She was due back Sunday morning. I was grateful I had something to do the night of the wedding. Dalton had planned a campfire for the last Saturday night of the summer. It was pretty much the same group as the night Allie came—minus Allie, of course—and Stevie had met a counselor named Rachel, a tall pretty girl, so the number was the same.

We went to the same site as well. There were a couple Dalton frequented, but this was his favorite. "This might be the last one ever," Dalton said, as the fire started to rise. "Stuart, how many beers have we tossed in these woods?"

"Enough, I guess."

"Don't be sad, Dalton," C.C. said. "Nobody likes you when you're sad."

"You're not feeling it, C.C.? You and Stuart aren't coming back, either."

"I'm feeling it. We had a good run here."

C.C. asked Martha if she planned on returning. Martha said she did. Stevie and Rachel would be back, too. When it was my turn to answer, I said I would, but I very much doubted it. Being here without Allie would make for a long, lonely summer.

The whole evening was subdued. We drank the beer, we cooked the dogs, and we smoked the weed, but it never took off. Dalton said Charlie was doing bad, really bad. That had something to do with it.

I walked back to the boys' camp by myself, thinking about Allie, how we had walked back together that night beside the grazing field for the horses, where I first told her I liked her. I wished I could have that over, the night she first kissed me lightly.

* * * * *

I finally saw Allie on Sunday at lunch. It was almost two whole days, an eternity. It was like seeing her anew, that gentle slope of her nose, the pleasing shape of her body. After lunch, during rest period, I heard about the wedding and saw her dress. We didn't have a whole lot of time. There were some half-full boxes on the floor of the infirmary, as the day I first met her. Allie was starting to pack things up.

After rest period on middle Sunday, the boys swam the girls at the boys' pool, because it had more bleachers than the girls' pool. It was another brutally hot afternoon. I was sitting on the grass in the shade of a tall pine watching the meet when I noticed the white pick-up. I saw it up at the boys' mess hall, and then it headed down the hill toward us. Stevie was driving, alone. Maintenance didn't work on Sunday, so this was a little unusual.

Stevie came right over to me. "Something's up," he said. "Dalton's been in the cornfield for hours. He won't come out."

"What do you mean?"

"I don't know, Jake. Just by accident, Uncs saw him going into the cornfield about eleven o'clock. You know, we don't cultivate on Sunday. Uncs called after him, but he just kept walking."

"Are you sure he's still in there?"

"His truck's there. He's not anywhere else on the farm... I tried calling for him. He won't answer. I figured maybe you or Stuart..."

I looked around for Stuart and didn't see him. I got in the white pick-up. When we arrived at the cornfield, Dalton's blue Ford was parked there. "You want me to hang around?" Stevie asked.

"No. I'll find him, if he's out there."

First, I stood outside the head-high cornfield and called Dalton's name. I didn't wait very long before I started in. The corn being as high and lush as it was, you could see down a row only about twenty or thirty yards. I just kept walking, every now and then calling out his name, each time with a lower voice. After a while, I stopped.

After maybe ten minutes of searching, I found him. His back was to me as I approached in the same cornrow. His clothes were drenched with sweat, and his blonde hair looked like a wet mop. I could see he was hoeing furiously.

"What's going on?" I asked.

"I don't want to talk, Jake."

I just stood there watching him. "You got water out here?" The afternoon sun was beating down. "Dalton, do you have *water* out here?"

He wouldn't answer. "I'm going to go get you some," I said. "I'll be back."

When I returned, he was pretty much in the same spot, so I didn't have to find him again. This time I approached him not directly from the rear but from the cornrow next to the one he was hoeing. I still stayed a little behind him, though, when I thrust the plastic milk-jug of water at him. He took it from me and took a big gulp from the jug.

When he was handing the jug back to me, I saw his face. At first, I couldn't believe what I was seeing. His blue eyes that always gleamed were bloodshot. His whole face was red, especially around his eyes, as if he had been crying. He looked exhausted, as if he hadn't slept in a week.

"What the hell happened?" I asked.

He went back to his hoeing. I stood there. Talking to him wasn't working, so I moved along with him in the adjacent cornrow for at least five minutes. I was wracking my brain trying to think of what could have happened between now and the campfire, where I had seen him last. The only thing I could think of was something with Charlie. I knew this was something more than Charlie.

Finally, Dalton let go of his hoe, in the middle of another ambitious strike, and dropped to his knees. He just kind of buckled to the ground, in a heap of exhaustion. Then he started sobbing with his hands over his face, and his entire body shook. I stepped behind him and rested my hand on his shoulder. That was all I knew to do.

For at least a minute I stood there with my hand on his shoulder, watching and listening to him cry. Finally, he stopped enough to speak. "I ran," he said, and then he dropped his hands from his face. "I ran away."

I didn't know what to say to it. I moved the water jug a little forward so he could see it, but he brushed it off. "I was taking back the cooler, and I heard something. I went around to the window... Father White was butt-fucking Timmy Campbell."

My stomach plunged. The first thing I thought was that Father White had 'borrowed' him one night during first period. It was almost too incredible to believe, but I believed it. I didn't doubt it for a moment.

"I didn't stop it," Dalton said, with disgust. "I heard Timmy screaming, and I ran away from it, and let him *finish!*"

He broke down crying again and covered his hands with his face. From my hand on his shoulder, I could feel the bile and misery pouring out of him. Just as it had been with Allie, the pain was coming from his very core, and I knew no amount of tears could purge his desolation. Finally, he fell all the way forward with his head to the ground. Looking down at him I saw the belt Timmy had decorated, Dalton's name emblazoned.

At long last, he stopped, and then he said, "I don't want anyone to know what I did. Not Stuart. Not *anyone.*"

I offered the water jug again, and he took it. He drank about half a gallon. I stepped around him to pick up the hoe. "Let's get out of here. All right?" I held out my hand to help him up, and he took that, too.

We walked out of the cornfield together; I led the way. I tossed the hoe in the back of Dalton's pickup, but we didn't go anywhere. Perhaps he didn't know where to go now. We just sat there. Then he told me the wheels were in motion. Martha had called her father, and her father had already spoken with the Archbishop. The Archbishop had agreed to a meeting. "What was I going to do, go to Bernie?" Dalton asked.

"Is Martha okay?"

Dalton shook his head. "Not really. I didn't tell her everything, but I had to tell her, to talk to the old man."

We drove up to the barn, and then sat there again. Dalton wanted my advice. "What am I supposed to do about Timmy? Am I supposed to say something to him about it?"

"Christ," I said. "I don't know. I don't think so. No. The Archbishop needs to clean up this mess. Not you."

We sat there a while longer. "I went to see Father White this morning," Dalton said. "I told him I knew, and that if I ever saw him near that kid again, I was going to kill him."

* * * * *

Both Sunday nights of a period meant fried chicken, by far the best meal of the week. I barely ate a bite. In the mess hall, the first thing I did was walk to the other end to look at Timmy Campbell. He was smiling and talking to the kid next to him. I didn't think I could feel any worse when I entered into the mess hall, and of course, I did, when I saw him, that innocent little boy and that unspeakable act. Father White was not in attendance. Nor was Dalton. When I saw Allie, all I could hope was that she would never learn of it.

As we were leaving the mess hall, Allie came up to me and said, "You're coming tonight, right?"

It struck me as a little unusual she would have to ask. "Just as soon as cabin-walk begins."

When I entered into the infirmary, she gave me a big hug. "I'm so glad you're here," she said. We sat at her desk, which was usually where we started out. "Something is going on with Martha and Dalton," she said. "C.C. and I are worried sick."

I could see how it looked, what they were thinking. I didn't know what to say to it.

"Martha asked C.C. to watch her kids this morning.
She and Dalton were up at Charlie's house for a couple
of hours. Martha said they were using the phone. Who
the heck are they calling on a Sunday morning? What
else could it be? C.C. asked her straight out, and she
says she's not pregnant, but what else could it be?
Stuart told C.C. that Dalton looks like death warmed
over."

I took a moment to consider it. "She's not pregnant."

"How do you know? You know what's going on?"

"Yes."

She let a moment pass. "And you're not going to tell
me?"

"No."

"I don't like secrets," she said.

"It doesn't concern you, Allie. Something happened last
night, and the situation is being handled."

"And Martha's not pregnant?"

"She's not pregnant."

"Thank God."

It was raining hard outside. We played maybe three
games of backgammon at her desk, and I was glad for
the distraction. Allie loved winning as much as I hated
losing. She would help me some with my moves to teach
me, but not too much, not if it was going to cost her a
victory. I beat her once all summer.

Later on, we went to her back room, where we lit a
candle and turned out the light. We always talked before,
sitting on her bed together, which I liked almost as
much. "Do you want to get married?" I asked. Her eyes
popped. "Calm down. I'm not proposing. I mean, in
general, do you want to get married and have kids? We've
never talked about it."

"Why are you asking that?"

"In the years to come, I'll be thinking about you. Should I imagine you as a married woman with kids, or a career nurse?"

"I hope to get married and have kids."

"How many?"

"Maybe three."

"That sounds like a good number to me, too," I said. "Let's say you could have just one. Which gender would you choose? I know the answer."

"What?"

"A boy."

She smiled. "And you'd want a girl, wouldn't you?"

"I think you get more out of a girl," I answered. "Guys hit the bricks at twenty, and you never see them again."

We talked for a long while that night as the rain fell on the roof, the longest of the summer, about all sorts of things, places we'd like to travel or had been, more about our families. She told me again that I ought to be a writer, though we didn't dwell on it. I told her I didn't have anything to write about, and if I wanted to, I could spend a legal career writing.

When we were holding each other underneath the covers, I told her how glad I was to be with her tonight. "This thing that happened, it's really bad?" she asked.

"Yeah. It's as bad as can be."

* * * * *

The following day, Dalton and Martha left camp at two o'clock for their appointment with the Archbishop, about a twenty-five-minute drive to the main office of the Archdiocese downtown. Just before dinner, I walked over to the barn. Dalton was back in his work clothes. He was fixing a lawnmower that was propped on top of a garbage can. He looked much, much better today, but if you knew him, you could still tell he was a little off.

"What happened?" I asked.

"It went good. Good."

Dalton said they met Martha's father outside in the parking lot and were ushered immediately into the Archbishop's ornate office. Martha didn't go in with them. She went to another room and waited by herself.

"How long were you in there?"

"About a half hour. The Archbishop couldn't have been nicer. I mean, when you think about it, I'm talking to this guy twenty-four hours after we reported it. They're taking it seriously."

All of a sudden, I had a queasy feeling in my stomach. I didn't say anything. I let him continue. "I told him exactly what I saw. He was blown away. He was thunderstruck."

"Did he believe it?" I asked.

"Yeah. He didn't question it."

"What did he *say?*"

"They're going to take care of it, Jake. The Archbishop gave me his word. Father White is in big trouble."

"*Big trouble?* He should be rotting in jail for twenty years. Are they getting him out of here?"

Dalton paused. "I don't think they are. There are only a few days left in camp. You know they just want the summer to end quietly."

"Who cares what they want? No, they have to be getting him out of here."

"I agree with you. Even Martha's father was surprised. The Archbishop said he'll never be the director of Fort Ross again."

Now, I was the one thunderstruck. "They're not getting him out of here? You're kidding me, right? They're not pulling him out of this camp?"

"The Archbishop is responsible for the big picture. I know it isn't right. But he doesn't see it that way."

"What did Martha's father say?"

"He's the one who asked the question. He didn't like it, either, but he didn't challenge it... They're going to take care of it, Jake. These are holy men dedicated to God. You got to believe they're going to take care of this."

"We ought to call the cops," I said, though neither of us seriously considered it for a moment. I might as well have said we ought to fly to the moon.

* * * * *

After talking to Dalton, I was glad I had a couple of hours before I would see Allie at the infirmary. I absolutely could not believe that Father White was spending another night at Fort Ross, but he was. Allie knew me so well. I was determined to keep it all from her. When I stepped inside the infirmary, I could see she was making considerable progress packing up. More boxes were on the floor, and half the glass cabinets were empty. The strangest thing of all was that Bob Dylan wasn't playing. It was dead quiet.

"How about some backgammon?" I said. "Before I leave this place, I'm going to beat you one more time." I took my usual chair at her desk.

"Maybe later," Allie said. She took her chair across from me. "Father White hasn't been in the mess hall in two days."

My heart sank. She was studying me. I sat there trying to look innocent, all the while knowing I was guilty as hell. "This bad thing that happened, you said it was

Saturday night. Father White hasn't been in the mess hall since. Is that a coincidence?"

"I can't tell you," I said.

"Where did Martha and Dalton go this afternoon? Martha's father knows the Archbishop. That's where they went, isn't it, to talk about Father White? You said this thing was as bad as can be. What did he do, Jake? I want to know."

I looked down at the top of the desk. I couldn't look at her. The last thing I wanted to do was tell her, the very last. "You don't want to know," I said.

"I think I have a pretty good idea... Tell me, Jake. I know anyway. He molested a kid, didn't he?"

My eyes stayed down on the desk. I knew I had no choice, but I still couldn't bring myself to do it. Perhaps ten seconds passed, before I raised my eyes to her and said, "Timmy Campbell."

"Oh, God."

"After the campfire, Dalton was returning the cooler when he heard something-"

"What do you mean *heard?*" Allie asked quickly. "Oh, God. Oh, *God!!!*"

I never intended on telling her, which is why I did such a rotten job at it. I certainly never intended on giving her the full picture, which I had inadvertently done. Allie about jumped out of her chair and started pacing in a brisk manner, around the boxes on the floor to start out.

I sat there in mortification over the way I had handled it. Allie paced as far as the entrance to her room, and then she came back to the desk. I don't know how many times she made that same path—ten, maybe. Her face was red and twisted, and you could just feel the intense anger and unbounded rage surging inside her.

Finally, I took her gently by the wrist. "Will you just talk to me?"

I could feel her try to pull away at first, but I held onto her, and she gave in. I stood momentarily, to kind of deposit her into her chair. I sat back down, and nothing passed between us for a while. Without Bob Dylan, the silence was deafening.

"I'm sorry, Allie," I said finally.

"What happened with Dalton and the Archbishop?" she asked.

I prepared myself for round two. How was I going to tell Allie that Father White was here for the duration? A few hours before, I had been rebuking Dalton at the paucity of the response. Now was I in a position where I would have to defend it?

"They're going to take care of it," was my reply. "That was all the meeting produced. The Archbishop promised he was going to handle the situation appropriately."

"What does that mean?"

"I don't know what it means." I figured I had to say it. "They're not removing him, Allie. With just a couple days left, they're not taking him out, because it would look bad."

I thought she would get up and start pacing again. She just sat there, staring straight ahead. For a moment or two, it was as if I wasn't even in the room, or she was in a place far away from here.

"Martha's father is pissed about it, too," I said. "How can they just leave that guy here?"

"People in power do what they want," Allie replied.

We sat there a long while without saying anything. Backgammon seemed ridiculous, as did anything else. "I should go," I said finally, and she agreed. I stood, and she remained seated. "I wanted you *never* to find out about this."

"I know you did," she said sadly.

Chapter Six

Allie didn't make it to the Tuesday mixer, the last regular mixer, due to a camper staying over. Friday night was the last mixer, and that was for awards. Dalton was chairman of the all-seeing, all-knowing Awards Committee. Three guys and three girls made up the committee. The event was conducted like the Academy Awards, with nominations for each of about thirty categories, which included 'Sexiest Guy' and 'Sexiest Girl in Camp.' Another was 'Loving Cup,' for the two people who absolutely hated each other the most after ten weeks of being fenced in. 'Loving Cup' was usually the most anticipated category, and one of a few decided by the voice of the mob, not the Committee.

On Wednesday, Father White appeared in the mess hall for dinner. I almost couldn't believe it, but there he was, sitting across from Allie. For me, it was the longest meal all summer. I don't know how Allie could sit there, but she did. I caught up with her as soon as we were outside. "You ought to eat in the girls' camp from now on," I said.

She didn't seem that phased by this new situation. "Maybe I'll go down there once, to say good-bye," she said. "Bernie does all the talking, anyway."

On Wednesday night, another camper stayed over at the infirmary. I saw the kid. From where I was standing, she didn't look very sick. I just got the feeling this kid didn't absolutely need to stay over. I didn't say anything. I could feel Allie pulling away from me. She knew better what was coming with us separating than I did, so I deferred to it. But it hurt.

Thursday night, at last, we sat at her campfire. We rolled out her trusty blue sleeping bag and put part of it over the tree trunk so we could lean against it with our legs stretched out. "I could get through the winter," she said, "with all the firewood you got me. Somebody needs to tell the next nurse this is back here."

"Stevie will be head of maintenance next year. We should tell him."

"You won't be here to do it?" she asked.

"No."

"I understand very well why you say that. But you could meet a nice girl here next summer. This is a good place to meet someone."

"A girl as good as you?"

"I'm not a girl, Jake. I'm a woman. You can't forget that... What happened between us this summer, you can't compare to anything else. This summer was a puff of smoke, a puff of magic white smoke. You can't expect to ever see it again, no matter where you are

I suspected she was right. She knew a lot more about life and love than I did. I was in no position to challenge it. "That camper didn't look very sick last night," I said.

"She was sick enough," Allie replied.

We played one last game of backgammon, and she beat my brains out. I told her that in the game of baseball, which she so loved, there was such a thing as not showing the other guy up. Allie said she didn't have to worry about beanballs in backgammon.

When the fire was burning down, she said. "Listen, I've been thinking about how we're going to say good-bye."

"I don't want to talk about that," I said.

"We need to... Tomorrow night, after the awards, we'll make love one more time in my room, and then we'll say good-bye. And when we're finished saying good-bye, that's it. I want you to go to your cabin."

I could barely bring myself to think about it. "You don't want me to spend the night?"

"We have to draw a line somewhere, Jake. That's as good a place as any. We'll be with each other one last time in my room, and then we'll say good-bye."

"I can't see you on Saturday?"

"You can see me. But whatever we need to say to each other, we'll say in my room."

"If that's the way you want it," I replied. I just wanted to stop talking about it.

* * * * *

Friday morning Reveille was the last one of the summer. Already I was getting nostalgic, thinking back over the bleary-eyed mornings I had spent saluting the flag. Part of me wondered where the summer had gone. Another part of me knew where it had gone, and I couldn't have been happier about it, except that it was over. The idea of me not seeing Allie every day, I just couldn't fathom it.

As the week wore on, Dalton grew more to his normal self. I saw him picking up Timmy Campbell for a slop-run to the pigs. Dalton may have appeared back to normal, but I think what he saw that night was the most traumatic event in his life. From what I saw in the cornfield, I believed he would never be completely the same again.

As soon as cabin-walk began, I headed to the barn with Stuart. Stevie and Uncle Bob were there. Dalton had the beer cold, and Stuart lit a joint. "Me and Stuart, it's our last night of four years," Dalton said as the sun was setting. We sat in chairs just outside the barn in front of the big sliding doors, and a nice warm breeze blew— winds of change, I supposed.

Before the awards began, we had about twenty minutes of music and straight drinking time as the Awards Committee finalized its momentous decisions elsewhere. When Allie and Martha came in together, Allie had on the same sleeveless white blouse as on opening night. She said it was her "lucky shirt" now. She stayed right with me for the ten minutes or so before we took our seats. As soon as she saw me, she kissed me on my lips and took my hand for a little while.

C.C. was a member of the Committee, so she didn't sit with us. Allie and I took our places on the shuffleboard table with our backs against the wall. Martha sat next to Allie, and Stuart was next to me. We had an excellent view from the shuffleboard table. Folding chairs had been brought over from the mess hall, which lined the entire floor of the basement. At the center of the long concrete wall across from us was a podium with a microphone. Behind the podium were two tables on which sat white Styrofoam cups turned upside down. On top were glued gold and silver trophy cups. A white envelope was below each Styrofoam cup.

Dalton led the Awards Committee in, ringing a playground bell. You could hear them coming from fifty yards. With the sound of the bell, the last few folding chairs were taken. I didn't see anyone standing. Dalton was wearing a T-shirt tuxedo and a black bowtie. I suppose it was custom for them to be booed, because they were booed soundly as they filed in.

Dalton stepped to the microphone. "The Awards Committee would like to thank the whole staff for coming tonight," he began. "We'd also like to thank all the foreign correspondents in attendance." He nodded to them. "Couldn't do it without you, guys."

It was good to see Dalton back again. I squeezed Allie's hand for no reason in particular. I was just glad to be with her.

"What this night is about," Dalton said, "is all you people who thought you got away with something, well, let me tell you." He wagged his forefinger. "*You didn't...* Tonight it all comes out in the wash."

The first category was by tradition 'Best Last-Night Hook-Up,' as if to underscore that no evening in a Fort Ross summer was exempt from the purview of the Awards Committee. Of the nominees, only a couple were from the present staff, which caused mild laughter. When Dalton announced the last nominees, however, anyone who wasn't a rookie burst out in surprise, laughter and applause. Of course, I had no idea who they were, but it had to be an unusually unlikely, outrageous pair.

Dalton nodded vigorously and raised his right arm as if to testify. "It's the God's honest truth... Ben and Susan, I don't know where you are tonight, but we got you!" He tossed their trophy over his head behind him.

In about the fifth category, Martha won for 'It's Nice to Be Naive.' C.C. presented it to her. Martha went to the podium, looked at her cup, and asked, "What does this mean?" She was happy as she returned to her place next to Allie, holding her trophy. "It's nice to win something."

When it was Dalton's turn to present again, he held up the envelope and announced 'Sexiest Girl In Camp.' The guys started clapping and whooping. This was one where, more or less, the crowd decided. The Awards Committee announced five names and decided only if there was a dispute.

The first two Dalton announced got generous support. Allie Smith was the third, and she eclipsed them by a wide margin. I was clapping my hands as hard as I could until they hurt. "Oh, God," Allie said. I knew she was enjoying it, and also that she didn't want to win. The fourth one announced didn't clearly beat her, either, but the fifth, a red-haired goddess named Maggie Gallagher, did. "That was a close one," Allie said, laughing with relief.

"You were *robbed.*"

C.C. handled 'Sexiest Guy In Camp.' The first name she announced was, "Dalton Talbott. He made us nominate him." The girls just about booed him out of the basement.

When the commotion finally died down, Dalton called out from his chair behind the podium, "Hey, I can put it on my resume!" More boos.

The girls gave a clear-cut winner as well. Needless to say, it wasn't Dalton, or me.

C.C. and Stuart were nominated for 'Couple of the Year' but didn't win. The next category was 'Late Bloomers,' for couples who got together toward the end of the summer. Stevie and Rachel were nominated. Allie and I won. We went to the podium together, but we didn't have to say anything. As with the 'Couple of the Year' nominees, all we had to do was kiss, and the crowd was satisfied.

Of course, the later the night got, the drunker and louder the crowd became. Dalton still had a couple of good ones for the end, I was sure. We still hadn't done 'Loving Cup,' the ultimate crowd-decider. I just had a feeling something was coming when Dalton again stepped to the podium with his famous grin.

"Our next category we've always called 'Corruption of Youth.' That's a pretty good name for it, don't you think? Well, the Awards Committee, in its infinite wisdom, has come up with a better one. Henceforth, and for here after, the title of this category will be forever known as... 'The Mrs. Robinson Award.'"

The whole basement erupted in laughter. When I looked to Allie, she was laughing as hard as anyone.

Dalton read the nominations. "Allie Smith. Allison Smith. Nurse Smith. Allie." He furled his arm toward her. "Here's to you, Mrs. Robinson."

Allie laughed her way to the podium. She composed herself once she reached it. She accepted her trophy from Dalton, and then said with a sly grin, "Since you all like movies so much, I've just got one thing to say: Some like it hot!"

I thought the roof might come down.

Allie came back and sat next to me as if she was proud to do so. "You got them," Martha said to her. "You got them *all.*"

I looked at Allie's trophy and held her hand. "You are the best girl in this whole camp," I said, turning to her. "And you're mine."

"Thank you, Jake... Thank you."

For just a few more hours, we still belonged together.

We cheered together in the 'Loving Cup' category, and that was the last one. The place cleared out pretty quickly after that, for anyone already with a mate. I just caught sight of Dalton and Martha as they were leaving. Martha was carrying her trophy. Some of the trophies made it out of the basement, but most didn't. Allie and I decided we would leave ours behind. "If I take it," I said, "I'll be moving it around until I'm sixty." Many were in a garbage can on the way out. We didn't go that far. We just left them behind on the shuffleboard table where we had sat, two upturned Styrofoam cups that said 'Late Bloomers' and 'Mrs. Robinson' side by side.

When we reached the infirmary, it came as something of a shock, because it was altogether shut down now. The mattresses on the two beds were shorn of covers. There were no boxes anywhere. All of the glass cabinets were empty.

Allie seemed to know what I was thinking. "I left my room exactly the same."

She did. She hadn't packed anything in here. Bob Dylan was still hanging. Her stereo hadn't moved. Most importantly of all, it smelled exactly the same. "I'm going to miss the smell of this room," I said, as we entered. "I'm going to remember it until I'm an old man."

We sat on her bed in our usual places, Allie with her legs crossed at the head of it, while I leaned against the wall at the base. "Well," she said, "you're no longer a virgin. Any regrets?"

"Are you kidding me? Because of how it happened, some people live their lives dreading the question. I can't wait. I lost it to a knockout nurse who was twenty-six years old. I'm thinking of taking out a billboard."

"Twenty-seven, technically... Does that make it better, or worse?"

"Can I ask you something? Am I going to get a phone number from you, or at least an address?"

She shook her head.

"I didn't think so."

"It's best I'm going so far away. Something like this, Jake, you just have to stay completely away from it. It only hurts more when you don't, and it doesn't do you any good."

I didn't say anything to it. I knew she wasn't going to change her mind, and also that she was probably right, as she usually was. "You're going to meet some girl in a dorm at Ohio State and forget all about me, that old hag."

"I think I'll do better with girls now, because of you."

"You will, Jake. Just stay exactly as you are."

We talked about the day we met. I didn't know until now that Allie and Martha had seen it all with the bees, from the moment of the attack. Allie told me it was her last drink of Vodka, and she was still embarrassed by it. "I kind of limped into this place," she said. "But I'm not limping out."

"I was your first since it happened, right?"

"Yes. I wasn't sure I would ever want to. Or I was afraid to. And then I met you... And you wouldn't leave me alone."

"We both helped each other, I think. That's what it comes down to, and we should be grateful for it. That puff of magic white smoke, it was real, Allie, for as long as it lasted."

We paused. She was looking at me with a sad smile. "Thank you for what you taught me," I said. "That's what I want to say to you. I'm not going to settle for anything less than what I found with you... I will always love you."

Her green eyes glistened. "You are a gift from God," she said simply, and didn't follow for a while. "In many ways, you've given my life back to me."

I smiled. "Not bad for a kid, huh?"

"You goof... No matter what happens, Jake, no matter what happens, I will love you until the day I die."

"Promise?" I asked.

"Yes."

After that, it seemed there was nothing more to say. I didn't want it to be over, but I knew it was. I tried to keep hold of it just a little while longer. I smiled. "Do you love me more than Bob Dylan?"

"Yes. More than Bob Dylan... Are you ready, Jacob?"

"Not yet," I answered. "I want to get one thing straight. I still get to see you tomorrow, right? If I go to my cabin tonight, I still get to see you tomorrow."

"Yes. You can see me tomorrow. That I promise, too."

Allie put her bare feet on the floor next to mine, and I started with the top button of her white linen blouse. "Thanks for wearing it," I said. "This is my lucky shirt, too."

"I figured you would appreciate it. You might have gotten underneath that night, if you hadn't been such a boy."

We proceeded as we had the first night we made love. Allie discarded her bra to the floor and then stood, so I could draw down her shorts. She took off my shirt and then sat down next to me. We were passionate that night, the most we had ever been, a raw primal ache that demanded to be sated, as if it ever could be. It was the energy of what she had released in me, and I had released in her, I think. I wasn't a total kid anymore, and she wasn't afraid, and we loved each other. It was very much different than our first night together, of course, and very good, but nothing could ever compare in my mind to that first night we made love.

We held each other under the covers for maybe fifteen minutes without saying a word. I think I was afraid to talk, because I knew what was coming. "It's time for you to go," she said.

"Already?"

"Yes."

I didn't argue. I slipped out of her arms and out of her bed. She watched silently as I pulled on my clothes. I sat down on the bed to put on my sneakers, and she placed her hand in the middle of my back and moved it softly.

When I was finished tying my sneakers, I stood. "I'm not saying good-bye," I said. "I'll see you tomorrow, or a couple hours from now."

"Good-bye, Jacob. Good-bye."

I turned and walked out of her room. I heard her crying before I reached the screen door.

* * * * *

I don't think I slept a minute that night. I sat on the porch of my cabin when I reached it, for at least a half hour. Eventually I went inside and stretched out on my bunk. It was a long while before I even closed my eyes. Sleep was something for another night. I went over every minute we had spent together in the summer, and by the time I was finished, I heard the first morning birds singing.

The bugle sounded at seven-thirty. There was no Reveille line-up on Outgoing Saturday, or breakfast. By eight o'clock the parents were arriving to pick the campers up. They had until eleven o'clock, but almost all campers were gone by ten, and it was a hectic two hours.

The parents of boy campers drove up to the boys' camp to collect the child and his steamer trunk in the baseball field in front of the stable. The parents of girl campers pulled to the front bonfire field just inside the main gate. The girls' steamer trunks were transported down by maintenance, with guy counselors loading and unloading.

Helping carry the steamer trunks to the baseball field was the last official act for a counselor. After saying farewell to my kids, I was assigned with others to clean the nine-and-a-half, the main shower and restroom facility. Because it was the last day, Bernie said we really ought to clean it for once, and good. Everybody was moving slowly after the big night. Nobody was saying anything as we doused the place with chlorine and started swabbing.

The building had an outside portion in front with sinks and mirrors. I happened to be there when I saw Dalton's blue Ford heading toward us. Almost always Dalton drove the big cattle truck on incoming and outgoing days. It didn't surprise me, though, to see him in his truck on his last day.

"Get in," he said.

"What, I can't—"

"*Get in!*"

I yelled something to my mates inside, which I didn't know if they heard, and got in. Dalton hit the gas. He was always really good about driving slowly around camp. It certainly wasn't the case today. "Where are we going?" I asked.

"The barn, so we can see," he answered. "Father White is dead."

It didn't completely register at first. "What?"

"He's dead. Deader than a doornail."

I didn't say anything to it. I was shocked, of course, but I didn't let myself go any further than that.

We were now approaching the boys' mess hall. "I was driving up to the girls' camp for another load, and I heard a woman scream," Dalton said. "Sister Helen comes running out of Father White's house. She jumps into my truck and tells me to take her to the infirmary. As we're pulling away, some of the girls are coming out of the shack. She screams at them not to go into Father White's house."

It can't be, I was thinking. *It just can't be.*

"Sister Helen was hysterical. We picked up Allie."

We came in sight of Father White's house and swung right by it. Nothing appeared amiss there. Outside the girls' shack, about five girls were standing near the screened-in porch. "Bernie's in there now with Sister Helen and Allie. Bernie threw me out and said not to tell anyone. I told them. There's ten girls standing there wanting to know. I told them."

We ascended back up the hill to the barn. Dalton made a U-turn, and we sat there facing Father White's house, from about seventy-five yards away. "Those priests should be arriving in about ten minutes, I figure," Dalton said. "Sister Helen called downtown to the archdiocese. That's what Allie told her to do when she asked."

I still didn't want to believe it. I couldn't believe it.

"I went in with them," Dalton said. "There he was, lying flat on his back, with a huge red gash across his neck. His eyes were open, Jake. They were wide open." He paused for a moment, like he was remembering it. "There was blood all over the place. The knife was on the bed, the kind Lil gives out for cutting watermelon on overnights. She keeps those sharp."

I just sat there, incapable of speech. Even Dalton took a break for a moment, as we waited. "Jake, there's only three people who knew about Father White. You, me and Martha. I know Martha hasn't said anything. She's scared straight. Did you tell anyone?"

"No," I answered quickly. "No."

He laughed a little. "You didn't do it, right?"

"No."

"I guess it's a suicide then," Dalton said. "But it didn't look like one to me."

"What do you mean?"

"I don't know. The whole thing just didn't seem right. If you're going to kill yourself, why do it *that* way? You put on your pajamas, climb into bed and slit your throat? Not only that. I turned it off. His alarm clock was still blaring."

"What did Allie say?" As I asked it, I could hear myself asking.

"We went in. She touched the body and said it was cold. Sister Helen asked what she was supposed to do? Allie told her to call the archdiocese and let them notify the police. Sister Helen knew the number to call... They'll be here any second. The cops should be here already."

I sat there and tried not to think, because each thought was like movement in quicksand, with absolutely nothing to hold onto. I just kept sinking lower and lower. Every thought confirmed it, until I slipped below, all the way under into a black void. I could no longer deny it.

"You think she's still in there now?" I asked.

"Maybe," Dalton answered. "I don't know why Allie would need to stick around. Sister Helen is the one who found him. She's the one the cops will want to talk to. Allie doesn't know anything more than I do."

There was still plenty of traffic on the main road, but the first two-hour onslaught to the boys' camp was pretty much over with. A small, plain sedan pulled into Father White's driveway, and three priests emerged, all in black. They looked young.

"Okay, the priests are here," Dalton said. "Where are the cops?"

No more than a minute passed from when the priests entered and Bernie came out. Once I saw Bernie leaving, I was fairly sure Allie wasn't in there, either. When the cops arrived, most likely, only Sister Helen and the priests would be there to receive them.

"I gotta go," I said.

"Where? I'll take you."

"No. I want to walk."

I was aware of my first few steps out of Dalton's truck, almost as if I were checking to see if my legs still worked. When I hopped into Dalton's old Ford Pickup, I was one person. Walking away from it, I was another.

To get to the infirmary, I could have walked past Father White's house. I chose to walk behind Charlie's house, along the grazing pasture for the horses, to the baseball field, where the few remaining campers were mostly seated on their steamer trunks. At the boys' mess hall, I picked up the blacktop walk that led past the boys' office and to the playhouse. Once through the playhouse, it was grass to the infirmary. Probably it was a five-minute walk, five minutes to try to gather my thoughts, when I would need a lifetime.

I didn't knock on the screen door. I pulled it open, and she was waiting for me, seated at her desk. The inside of the infirmary now looked as empty and barren as her soul. She didn't look away from me as I was standing there. She didn't say anything for a while, but she didn't look away from me, either. Instead, she met me eye to eye.

"He's never going to do that to another little boy again," she said finally.

"I guess not," I replied. "I guess not."

"They weren't going to stop him. No one was going to stop him from doing it again."

"How do you know?"

"They wouldn't even take him out of this fucking camp. And it cost him his life, his pathetic miserable life."

"Who are you to judge?"

"Someone has to, when there is no law. People who live above the law need to accept justice as it comes. And it came to Father White."

"Dalton will be a suspect. He told me he threatened to kill Father White."

"No one is touching Dalton Talbott. Grow up."

"I think I just did. About twenty minutes ago."

"There's not going to be an investigation. At twelve o'clock, Bernie and Sister Helen will get on the loudspeakers, and everyone will go home."

"Dalton said it didn't look like a suicide."

"It looks *enough* like one. Right now, the Catholic Church is using all its weight to shut it down. Which do you think they want? Do they want a troubled priest who committed suicide? Or do they want a pedophile priest who was murdered at a Catholic camp? Power can change what it is, and it will... I could call the

Archbishop, tell him I did it, and he'd hang up on me. He's the one who left him here. They don't want to know."

"You sat there in the mess hall with Father White how many times this week?"

"Four," she answered, with ice in her voice. "And you know what I saw: A sitting duck. He didn't understand how vulnerable he was. And the very thing that protected him was going to be his downfall. I looked at him, and I sized up his neck. I wondered if his white collar would cover up where I cut at his funeral."

"Who *are* you?" I asked, with disgust.

She was defiant, her green eyes blazing. "No one was going to *stop* him! There's another little boy out there, or ten, or fifty, who are going to have their lives the way they're supposed to be. I'll meet my Maker on it. And maybe he'll show me those boys, those boys who lived their lives without being attacked by a monster."

"How could you do it?" I asked. "How could you laugh at the awards and then make love to me, all the while knowing what you were going to do in a few hours time?"

"I didn't know I was going to do it. I knew I was going to try. If he had locked his door, he'd be alive right now."

I looked at her a long moment, in utter despair. "What a cold, black heart you have," I said.

Those were the last words I ever said to her. I turned my back to her and walked out the screen door.

With the awareness of a zombie, and perhaps the pace, as well, I moved through the playhouse into the boys' camp. I went up the gentle hill along the nine cabins that ended at the nine-and-a-half, where my fellow counselors were probably still cleaning, and I kept on going, beyond the boys' tennis courts and into the woods. I kept waiting to wake up from it, the scariest nightmare of my life.

In the woods, I put one foot in front of the other and breathed a bitter brew of shock, emptiness and confusion. I could taste it, the bitterness in my mouth, and I knew no amount of water could wash it away. I had spent all summer on these trails, but the woods looked different to me today. I had never really appreciated how truly lush and green it was.

I kept on walking until I reached the power line at the back of the woods and saw the yellow and purple weeds that were once flowers. In the ankle-high grass, I stopped and dropped down to it, in the bright morning sun. I thought my skull might split from the headache that was throbbing. I tried my best to massage my temples, but there was nothing to assuage the discomfort. Never in my life had I experienced anything that was so big and so bad. I knew it was true, but I couldn't bring myself to accept it. Even after talking to her, I just could not bring myself to accept it as true.

I think I was out in the woods about forty-five minutes. By the time I made it back to the boys' camp, the whole staff was milling around the boys' office, in anticipation of getting paid. I was pretty sure Allie wasn't among them. She didn't get cash in an envelope on Outgoing Saturday as the rest of us did. I was looking for Dalton but got snagged by a couple of guys wanting to say good-bye. I stood and talked for a few minutes, mostly about the summer, and also about Father White. It was generally considered he committed suicide.

When I found Dalton, we walked a little away from the group so we could talk privately. "The Archbishop is here," Dalton said. "About a half hour ago, he pulled up in a big black Cadillac. The place is crawling with priests. There's one cop-car down there. *One.* You know they don't want a whole bunch of cop-cars on Outgoing Saturday."

I looked around at everyone saying good-bye. Father White's death may have added a little flavor to it, but it was nothing more than the last minutes of a Fort Ross summer. Where were the detectives to ask for names and alibis? They weren't coming.

"How did the summer end like this?" I asked.

Dalton shook his head in bewilderment at first, but then he recovered to his normal self. "It was a good summer, Jake. Yeah, it had a rocky end, but it ended as it should. If I got caught doing something like that, I'd slit my throat, too. It works out for the church. They have to tell Timmy Campbell's parents, but now at least they can say Father White has atoned for his sin. It kind of wraps it in a neat bow, except if you're Timmy Campbell."

I thanked Dalton for his friendship, for taking me in from the very first day. I told him I hoped to see him sometime again. "You will, Jake. You will."

I stepped in line to get paid. C.C. gave me a big hug while I was standing there. I thanked her, too, most especially for her advice. I said a special good-bye to Martha as well, before the girls headed back down to their camp.

After that I went to my cabin for my duffel bag, and I walked it to my car by the mess hall. I put it on the back seat, and then rested my one and only blue suit, which had been hanging, on top of it. Down deep, I supposed, I knew I was never going to wear that suit.

With a few minutes to go, we gathered around the boys' office again, this time without the girls. Perhaps because it was a much smaller group now, I was conscious of keeping my back to the playhouse and infirmary. There was a lot of handshaking. I made many good friends not mentioned in these pages. It was good to have these last few minutes to reminisce.

Bernie came over the loudspeaker. "All right, you knuckleheads, some of you have nine months before you're due back here. Some of you have the rest of your lives. Make the best of it."

As a group we walked toward the mess hall, where our cars were parked, and we started our engines. In a long column, I drove out with everyone else, past Father White's house. Among many others, the Archbishop's black Cadillac was parked there, and still one police car. *There wasn't going to be even a hint of an investigation,* I thought. We were the evidence of that, as we coasted down the hill, past the well at the girls' shack and out of the main gate.

After ten or fifteen minutes of driving from Fort Ross, I hit the suburbs of the city. I looked at the stoplights and the fast food joints as if from a Third World country, or from Mars. It was just so strange to be out of Fort Ross. I had felt it a little on the previous breaks, but today it was an overwhelming sensation. I was no longer there. I was no longer in that place, in that world. And that world was forever gone.

Chapter Seven

I've lived my adult life with the idea that I was complicit in the murder of a pedophile priest. Of course, I didn't plan it or do it, but it was because of me that Allie knew about Father White. And I sure didn't point a finger at her when it was over. There was another way I was complicit, as well. Over that summer, Allie became strong again, strong enough to do it, and part of that was due to me. I don't believe she would have done what she did had she not met me. Dalton's failure had an end to it, I hope for him. My guilt has never ended.

I did, indeed, meet a girl in my dorm at Ohio State— not 'the' girl, but a good one, and I probably could have married her, if not for Allie. I wasn't ready to settle for anything less. Ohio State turned out to be a fantastic experience. In my years there I was to witness the great Heisman runner, Archie Griffin, and the most legendary football coach in the program's vaunted history, Woody Hayes. (Sorry, Urban.) I went to some classes, too.

I met my wife, Karen, on a Saturday morning when I was twenty-eight years old. It was kind of a sketchy place, a tire store that was having a big sale. The store was overrun with customers and woefully understaffed. We went across the street and shared coffee while our cars were up on the racks. Karen was as good as Allie. That's all I need to say. Until now, she is the only one I've ever told this story to, and I told her almost right away.

It was the mid-seventies when the first real revelations came about the conduct of the Catholic Church concerning pedophile priests. If I didn't know before, I knew then that Father White undoubtedly would have moved on to other victims, and probably many more. Allie was right about that. In all the time I was with her, she was right on just about everything, except for the one big thing, and that was the most important of all.

Of course, the revelations and practices continued for decades. They were almost impossible to get away from. One day, when I was in my mid-thirties, I was sitting in a civil deposition when it occurred to me for the first time that Allie had probably used the firepit we had built her to burn her clothes.

In the mid-eighties, when I was thirty-six, I ran into Martha at a charity gala. She was dressed in black, and as pretty and elegant as ever. She saw me first. She came up to me with a big smile and threw her arms around me. "Gosh, Jake, is it really you?"

We sat at a table and talked for a long time. Martha had a little girl, and was exactly the same. "You know," she said, with a smile, "Dalton Talbott taught me a thing or two that summer." She said she still had her trophy for 'It's Nice To Be Naive.' "I won it again the next year, but I didn't keep that one... The Awards Committee is just *mean.*"

I knew that Stuart and C.C. had married. Presently, I learned Stuart was a dentist in North Carolina, where they had five kids. "C.C. says it's only half a cabin. It sounds like a lot to me."

Martha said she talked to C.C. about once a year. "C.C. gets Christmas cards from Allie, Jake. She has two boys. Two tow-headed boys, just as blonde as Allie. C.C.

says they are the most gorgeous things." Allie had married a doctor out there, I learned.

I didn't sleep that night, or even try to for most of it, and I didn't have to say why. Some wives would have been green with jealousy. Karen understood. Part of the reason she wasn't threatened by it, I hope, was because she knew I wasn't living my life thinking I should be with Allie. What Karen knew, and accepted, was there was a chapter in my past that would always be highly complicated and deeply emotional.

I saw Dalton some through the years. Let's just say he socialized in loftier circles than I did. I don't think he ever worked that much. Maybe once a week he wore a business suit. He traveled and played a lot of golf at his country club. When I saw him, though, he was the same old Dalton. I was a long-lost brother he had miraculously found.

Dalton became good enough at golf to qualify for many years in the city-wide tournament, which you could follow in the newspaper. One year he came in fifth. Just before the turn of the century, Dalton was in a small plane with three other guys that went down in a wooded area in Georgia, their destination for a weekend trip. It was a big news story in town, for the other three were prominent business executives as well. Mangled clubs and balls were scattered all over one gentle hillside.

I attended the funeral. Dalton left behind a devastated wife and a daughter and a son. Dalton Talbott was a good man who had the good sense never to complain about anything. Ever. He always saw the best. And when he made his big mistake that night by running away, he blamed no one but himself, and tried to right it as best he could. I consider him one of the best friends I ever had, however briefly.

One of my first years in office the name Timothy Campbell came across my desk, on a sexual assault charge. My clerk was about to leave for the day, and I held him up, something I rarely did, so he could check on the defendant's age. It wasn't Timmy. I have thought about him through the years but have never had the courage to actively investigate what became of him. I suppose the answer to that question I'm willing to let blow in the wind.

Once I saw Martha for the first time after camp, our paths crossed about every three or four years at some function or another. I loved seeing her. She might be the kindest, sweetest person I ever knew. In the summer of 2002, on an August evening about seven o'clock, I picked up the ringing phone in my study, where I am now, and Martha was on the other end of the line. All I had to hear was for her to say my name and identify herself, and I knew.

"Allie?" I asked.

"Yes," she answered softly. "I'm sorry, Jake."

Allie had died of breast cancer and was buried out there. One of her sons was in medical school. C.C. said she had been gone about six months.

Hanging up the phone, I thought about the last words I had said to Allie. I knew for sure now I would never get a chance to say another. I had always hoped that somehow, some way, I would get to see her again and those would not be the last words. Over the years I had thought about Allie more at Christmas than in the summertime. She had a sizeable family here. Maybe two or three times during the season I would hear "I Want A

Hippopotamus For Christmas" over the radio, and I would wonder if this was the year I might run into her at the local grocery—a Lloyd Christmas chance, to be sure, but at least it was a chance.

I sat for just a moment before I went into the kitchen to tell Karen. "She knows, Jake," Karen said. "She knows you loved her." Then she put her arms around me and started crying softly, for me.

* * * * *

In my study, alone, I put on Bob Dylan's "Tangled Up In Blue" and then reached down into the bottom drawer of my desk, which held just one item, an old tin container, a thin one, like the size for cigarettes. The container hadn't been opened in thirty years. It held the blue bandanna Allie had given me the first day we went riding.

I went into a depression that lasted weeks, until the summer was over. Depression was something I was prone to as a teenager, so I knew what it was, but I hadn't experienced it since. When the leaves started turning colors, I was better. Throughout it all, Karen was nothing but patient and kind.

* * * * *

On a Sunday afternoon in the summer of 2011, I went back to Fort Ross, or the property there. Karen was away for the weekend with her girlfriends. I'm not sure why I did it. I just got in my car and drove there. Fort Ross closed as a summer camp in 1989, partly due to lack of attendance and high operating costs. There was another factor as well. A couple miles from Fort Ross, the United States government had been producing since the Fifties elements for uranium at a super-secret site. Lawsuits were flying all over the place, and to the Catholic Church, Fort Ross was worth more as a casualty.

I heard that the entire thousand acres sold for half a million, but I'm sure much more was received from the government. For about fifteen years the property was owned by a successful restaurateur, who used it as a personal playground for his extended family. All the buildings remained. Then Fort Ross was sold to developers. The price I heard was five million. By then, the whole uranium scare was over with. Unfortunately for the developers, the purchase of Fort Ross came just before the crash of 2008. Maybe half the property was built upon, very nice homes, before they lost their shirts.

The old entrance was no more. Now it was someone's back yard. Houses were built there. I had seen the new main entrance coming in and eased past it. Driving into the subdivision, and starting without my bearings from the old entrance, I didn't recognize the place at all. So much earth had been moved it was impossible to recognize. The woods were all gone. You knew if you were way back where the woods used to be, or in the boys' camp or the girls', but that was about it. I really couldn't figure within five hundred yards where the infirmary had been.

It was on my way out that I saw it. The old barn was still there. Within seventy-five yards of it, houses were built, but the old barn was still standing there, all alone. Perhaps the developers used it for storage. It made sense to me that it would be the last building left. I got out of my car and put my feet on Fort Ross soil for the first time in about forty years, walking over to it. High weeds were growing all around the block foundation. Mostly the body was gray, but it still had some white paint, and you could still see some of the black paint, too—the big bold letters that said 'FORT ROSS.'

From the barn I had my bearings, and I could see where Father White's house had been—the front riding corral, the front bonfire field. When I was finished looking around, I turned my attention back to the barn. I stood there a long time in front of the massive sliding doors that were padlocked, waiting for Allie to come out, waiting for Dalton to stride out with that big grin and gleam in his blue eyes.

* * * * *

That summer was the great dividing line of my life, even more so than marriage. There was a before and after. Whether I would have become a judge or not, I don't know. Perhaps it had nothing to do with it, and perhaps it had everything. What I know is I've lived a good life with a good wife and two sons and a daughter that I love with all my heart. I try not to question things. I try to be happy for what I have.

I will always be grateful for that summer. Part of love is a time and a place, I believe. For Allie and me, however star-crossed, the time and the place were exactly right for us to fall deeply in love, and we gloried in it, in the ability to love, and in the ability to love again. Allie has never left me. I have never felt truly alone since the day I met her. I always knew there was someone out there who cared as much about me as I did her. I will love her always. I will love her until the day I die.

Well, Allie, wherever you are, you finally got me to write something.

Made in the USA
Lexington, KY
30 June 2019